Cortical Fields

Versions of the stories collected here were originally published in the following publications: "Salvage," in *Arroyo Literary Review*; "A Question of the Tide," in *Lowestoft Chronicle*; "Border Control," in *West Branch Literary Magazine*; "Your Mothers Must Come," in *Serving House Journal of Literary Arts*; "A Morning Swim to North Korea," in *The Wang Post*; "Cultural Revolution or Cultural Decapitation," in *The Wang Post*; "Flames on a Hot Day," in *KYSO Journal of Arts & Literature*; "Fresh Papers," in *Whistling Shade Literary Journal*; "Your Eternity," in *Fiction Fix Literary Journal*; "Imagicon Farm," in *Lowestoft Chronicle*; "Put Your Death in the News," in *Poydras Review*.

Cortical Fields

Stories by Victor Robert Lee

PERIMETER SIX PRESS

PUBLISHED BY PERIMETER SIX PRESS

Perimeter Six is an imprint of The Pacific Media Trust

www.perimeter-six.info

Library of Congress Control Number: 2018950864

ISBN 978-1-938409-09-7

eISBN 978-1-938409-10-3

First published in the United States of America

Printed in the United States of America

Cover design by Joseph Langdon

Dedicated to the freedom of lives and minds.

SALVAGE

Seven people of the island drowned that summer, but Isaac was not among them. The others were seized by a wave as they fished, or lost as they swam out to sun themselves on an islet of slate, or sucked down by a current that didn't belong there, where the water lapped at a well-known rounded boulder.

Isaac, little Isaac, was floating in a child's raft in hand-deep water while his mother sat just three steps away talking to another young woman on the beach. The low sun cast orange light everywhere, except on the graying surface of the sea. The sound of the women's conversation was like two rattles shaking, and soon it left Isaac's ears as the raft drifted out with the soft breeze and caught a surface current flowing south, toward Africa. The women's chatting was undisturbed by Isaac's departure; perhaps the shimmer of the sunset hindered their vision.

"Women—their talking eats them up," Simeon would say later.

Simeon heard the screams and slid down the rocky butte to the strip of sand, already seeing a spot that didn't belong there, near the horizon, a floating coin.

"Simeon!" The women were crying out and waving their hands, pointing to the sea.

"Isaac! Isaac!" Simeon shook off his sandals, ran, dove, swam.

Three-year-old Isaac was riding both the current and the wind, and after ten minutes of swimming, Simeon knew it would be a race against nature to save him. He settled into a heaving rhythm, occasionally lifting his head in mid stroke to see his mark. It seemed closer. It seemed farther away. He wasn't sure.

He threw his arms forward like spears with each stroke, then ripped them back as the rail of muscles from hand to hip on each side burned in its turn and was released. Each breath went out with a jetting *whoosh*, and as the rhythm intensified, he saw in his mind last week's bodies again. Two sons of a cousin, just becoming men, taken off a rock by the same wave and sucked under by the currents. It was seventy feet down where Simeon found them, wearing his diving tank. Eyes open, the boys' familiar faces were stoic, and their limbs spread-eagle. They looked like upturned starfish.

Maybe it was the late-day faltering of the breeze, or a slackening of the current, or the surge of desperation that filled Simeon's chest and set him churning faster; after almost an hour he reached the boy.

"Isaac, you are too fast!" Simeon sputtered and grasped the raft, careful not to indent the few inches of inflated rubber that kept the child from the sea. The boy prattled as Simeon looked into his brown eyes, searching the dark round planets. Then Isaac laughed.

Simeon pulled and stroked until the sky had turned to deep violet, and the man and boy reached the sandy-bottom shallows not so far down the coast. The young mother screamed the boy's name and rushed into the water, followed by Simeon's fiancée. Like the women's hysteria, Simeon's anger had ebbed during the long swim back. Now it surged again.

"What kind of mother are you? Are you trying to lose the boy?" He grabbed Julia's arms and shook her as she cried and hugged her son. "Any moment he could have fallen in. What were you thinking?!"

Her head was whipped around by his shaking. The other woman grabbed his arm to stop him.

"And you, Nina! Sitting there. Will you do the same with our babies?"

The three of them were still waist-deep in the water. At last the boy was crying. As Simeon plodded onto the sand, he said, "You see, now he cries in his mother's arms. When I reached him, he was laughing. A child of the sea, like me."

He left them. The women picked up Simeon's sandals in silence.

On the dock at sunrise the next day, Simeon could feel in the sluggishness of his body that he had not slept well. The four men, four who had grown up together, were quiet as they threw their gear onto the old cargo boat that during the war had shuttled to Malta the meager food that kept thousands from starving. A "lifeline boat," they had called it, always on the verge of sinking under its own overloading, or under gunfire.

Its bilge required constant pumping, but its engine never failed on the six-mile chug out to Filfla Island. Simeon's three friends had rigged the boat with a large winch to pull up the unexploded bombs that littered the seabed. Filfla had been the practice target for the British, and now the island yielded a precious grainy mash of explosives, which Simeon's friend Jonas knew how to harvest from the old bombs and package into loud fireworks for the celebrations of each village's patron saint. In the old times, a patron saint got a single day of feasting, but now the villages carried on their festivals for as many as five days, and none of these days was complete in a Maltese mind without continual explosions. It was common on a summer evening in the countryside to hear detonations from three or four celebrating villages at once.

They anchored near the island's sun-facing cliffs, blindingly bright at this hour. Simeon wanted only to hunt rays and bream and eels and octopuses, but he couldn't shake off the chiding and pleading of his friends; he was the only diver, the only one among them born of dolphin sperm, they said. They had to force him to take money for his work, because diving for him was not work. His share of the money was small because, unlike the others, he had no taste for the onshore drudgery of scraping and rolling and wrapping, turning a man into a factory. More than that, he had no taste for what they produced—little grenades of pointless idolatry.

On a dive a few days before, he had seen an oblong shape shadowed by the crevice in which it was lodged. Simeon hadn't told the others of the blurry find. He'd only said, "I think there is more, to this side, for next time."

He found it again on the first dive, a bulky silhouette. He came up for a marker buoy and eighty feet of steel cable, saying nothing of the size, only, "If I can get the loop around it, it will be heavy."

The bomb was wedged with its nose pointing down, half wrapped in sea moss and so tightly gripped by the rocks that the figure eight of cable with which Simeon usually hitched the front and back would not pass around the nose.

5

He ascended and called for the pick hammer. He went down again, chipped away some stone, and slipped the noose over the troublesome front end of the bomb.

Back on the surface, it was a struggle for Simeon to get into the boat, even with his friends' arms hoisting him. He felt unsteady as he slid the tank down to his side and pulled off his fins. The winch took up the slack and the engine stammered, jerking the cable. The load responded to the steady pull. But then the engine suddenly whined, and the cable started spinning loose around the winch drum. The bomb had slipped out.

Tariq stiffened in fear of a blast. Jonas and Nico laughed at his panic.

"Don't worry, little Tariq!" said Nico. "They're like old men—no more spark left."

"Maybe it's better to let this one get away," Simeon said as the others readied the line for another try.

Jonas put his hands on Simeon's shoulders, squeezing the dense muscles and rocking him back and forth. "But Simeon, he's too big to let him get away."

On the next dive, Simeon saw that the bomb had cleared the crevice, and now sat on a jumble of rocks with many gaps available for the cable to be threaded through. He made his loops, checked the metal clips again, and took his time ascending. The sun was higher now and made the underwater landscape glare, erasing its deep blues. He would never hunt at this time of day, preferring sunrise or dusk, when the colors were just coming to life or slipping away, and the glints of light made sharper tears in the water's violet curtain.

The three hauled it in as Simeon sat and drank from a sun-warmed beer bottle. Jonas had to swing the crane arm to the stern because the boat listed too sharply when they tried to bring it over the gunwale. Even Nico worried that the rusty arm would crack under the weight.

But there it sat, shiny in its coat of gelatinous sea lettuce, as long as the men were tall.

More beers went around. The men were all sweating; there was no wind. Jonas, the ringleader, sat on the prize, nearly slipping off because of the slime. He pretended to ride it like a horse, yelping. Its girth was so great that his feet did not touch the deck.

He dismounted and held his bronze arms wide to hug Simeon.

"Simeon! One day you save my baby, and the next day you give me a new one."

At the dock, they finally got the bomb onto a dolly. Simeon left as the other three pushed it across the packed yellow dust to a shack in a walled enclosure, their workshop. The day's task was over. Opening the big catch and removing the filling would have to wait another two days, until after the town's feast of Our Lady of Pompeii. It was only afternoon and already the rumbling fireworks of another village's celebration could be heard miles away.

The next day, the main square of Marsaxlokk and all the narrow lanes leading to it were draped with flags and banners. Bright greens, loud yellows, and red crosses of the Knights in a dozen permutations. Families sat in a sprawl of wooden tables and chairs in the streets, the kids chasing each other, an occasional four-year-old dancing to the clangs and trumpet screams of the makeshift bands in the parade of mannequin saints. The cracking booms of the afternoon fireworks echoed off the old limestone façades.

Simeon sat alone at one of the outdoor tables, and through the din he did not hear his friends calling his name. Tariq came up from behind and gave him a slap on the back. He pulled up a chair, his face reddened by the grappa and beer. Nico and Jonas and a few others walked over and leaned on the tables.

"Nico, what about that one, the one named Sylvia?" said Tariq, nearly shouting. "She's got no one; no one in sight anyway. Maybe she'll like you even with that nose of yours."

"She's some cousin of Simeon's, right?" Nico was interested.

"You know, we're all related," said Simeon. He was distracted, trying to overhear the sunburned man with the tight British accent two tables away.

"Arab blood and Catholic rites, with too much Sicily mixed in ... ," was all Simeon could make out. The war had brought the British as soldiers; now the noisy spectacle of saints brought them as tourists.

"Yes, all related, even if we don't know it." Tariq was giddy. "One man's wife is another man's—" Another loud boom cut Tariq off. A sprinting kid spun around a chair, grabbing Simeon's sleeve to stop himself from falling down. Simeon scrubbed his hand on the boy's head.

"A natural-born father," laughed Tariq. "Too bad you lost your chance with Julia."

"No loss. My best friend got her." Simeon raised his beer bottle at Jonas. "Like family."

Tariq jumped up. "Hey, Nico! If you get that Sylvia— better chain her to your bed or she might hop in with Jonas!"

Jonas clamped his arm around Tariq's neck and squeezed. "Enough of the old times. You single guys will choke on your own balls."

Tariq struggled, trying to breathe, and he and Jonas fell on Simeon, knocking him and his chair to the ground. Tariq jerked himself out of the suffocating neck hold, sending Jonas's elbow into Simeon's head. Simeon responded with a fist to Jonas's face, and then the two of them were punching each other and grappling on the paving stones, covered with dust and liquor and smashed bread. They collided with chairs and knocked over a table before their friends dragged them apart. Blood was dripping out of Simeon's nose; Jonas's right eye was already swelling shut.

The two stood panting, glaring at each other, until Simeon walked away.

He wandered along small lanes, the dusk settling in and the explosions unbearably loud. "We'll all go deaf, or worse," he said out loud. "For a bunch of saints."

"Simeon Azzopardi! Having a nice talk with yourself? Well then, try not to argue!" The widow Fiteni cackled with laughter. She had been sitting on a nearby porch and now stood up feebly.

"It's sure," she said.

"What is sure?"

"Your big find; the boys scraped it off and it's the same. The same as the one that dropped in on the church. The bomb that in all his goodness the Lord made a dud. How they could drop it on a Sunday evening, knowing we were all there . . . and no one was killed, not a one."

Everyone knew the story. During the war, a German half-tonner had crashed through the church dome in Mosta, up the road, when Mass was just beginning. It thudded on the marble floor and rolled, but didn't explode. There were plenty of broken bones, but no one died, unless you counted widow Fiteni's husband, whose femur got cracked. He bled to death, but it was slow, so he didn't expire until three days later. She didn't count that.

"Maybe my buddies will give the bomb shell to the church, to put on display up there with the other one," he said, his voice sour. "After they get the powder out and get rich."

Simeon walked through the zigzag of narrow streets in an arc around the village center. The back lanes were empty except for cats and dogs wandering in and out of the glows of candles mounted on windowsills. He turned a corner and almost ran into two young women.

"Happy saint's day to you," said Julia. She was walking with a girlfriend, arm in arm.

"And to you."

"You've been fighting?"

"Just a scuffle. With the boys." A moment passed.

"Simeon, thank you for bringing Isaac back. I...," Julia's voice faltered and she lowered her eyes. The girlfriend strolled on by herself.

"He's too happy on the water," Simeon said. Then he frowned. "Are these from me?"

Julia followed his gaze to the bruises on her arms. Her face reddened in the candlelight but she said nothing.

"I'm sorry for doing that. Too much feeling for the boy."

"Simeon—I am sorry."

"Sorry you switched beds?"

"No! I am not." Julia folded her arms across her chest and took a step toward him. "What kind of life would I have with you, always in the water, having your fun? And a little shack. Nina can have it."

"Your love is for a big house then?"

"I loved *you*, Simeon." Julia kept her voice lowered. "You know I did. You know I wanted to spend every minute with you. But you would rather spend your time out there diving, playing, finding just enough fish for the next meal. Jonas is a good father," she said, sharply nodding her head.

"*Father.*" Simeon spat the word. "*Father?* There is just as much chance that *I* am his father, and you know it."

"No! It's not you. I'm sure." There was another cracking boom followed by a chorus of loud pops.

He tried to grasp her hand but she lunged away.

"Julia!"

She ran toward the cigarette ember of the other woman down the lane, and the two disappeared in the darkness.

In the morning, Simeon went up to Nina's house. Her father was slapping an octopus on the top of a stone wall, next to a mound of bougainvillea and morning glories in shades of pink and orange and dark purple. The brilliant pink was a color he never saw in the sea; he stared at it. The clap of the octopus rebounded off the wall of the house. Nina appeared in the doorway and took Simeon's hand as he approached.

"I looked for you at the *festa*," she said.

Simeon shrugged. "The guys and I made a little scene. Just as well you missed that."

"I heard. Why do you fight with your friends?" They were still holding hands. She had a jasmine flower and pressed it to his nose.

"It was no fight. We were just celebrating, like all the rest. I'm going for a swim. Maybe you'll have a big *sargu* to cook this afternoon."

"Tariq said Jonas wants to open it today. The bomb. They can't wait."

"Better than another fight in the square." He kissed her on both cheeks and said goodbye to her father as he walked down toward the shore. It was sunny, as always in the summer.

"We'll bury the *sargu* in garlic," she called after him. Simeon waved back. "Don't let the mermaids seduce you," she added more softly.

He entered the water and glided through it. When he reached the patches of sea grass and rippled sand that lay just before the drop-off, his eyes were teased by a hand-size flatfish skidding over the fine-grained seabed, the kind he had learned as a child to catch by snapping out his hand to pin it to the sand. Simeon let his speargun fall, swam toward the speckled fish, and dove down. When at last he had it, wriggling between his hand and the sand, and he was running out of breath, he heard a sharp, tinny smack. The concussion that rocked the water a moment later made him recoil with the dread of the air raids of his childhood.

The fish fluttered away from Simeon's loosened grasp. Simeon pushed off the bottom, his eyes filled with the vastness of the blue void beyond the drop-off. As he rose, he twisted so he would be facing land when he reached the surface. The cloud of black smoke and brown dust was still billowing from the site of the workshop, and a whole corner of the bay was in shadow. Simeon stroked violently toward the nearest land, a spit of rocks that slashed his feet when he climbed out and ran across them. It was hard to get close, through the choking dust, over the sharp-edged rubble. And when he got close, there was only the crater.

He had to back up a long way from the crater before he found pieces of them. They were such close and long-familiar friends that he could even distinguish whose shoulder it was, and whose knee, and whose foot. Hands, when he found them, at a greater distance, were the easiest of all.

"*Mama. Mama.*" It was a small voice, and it came from behind the exploded wall that had rimmed the work yard. Little Isaac was covered with large broken stones, one of which had nearly cleaved his right leg just below the knee. Simeon unburied him and squeezed a hand around the tiny thigh to keep the rest of the blood from running out.

"*Mama. Mama.*" Simeon stood holding the boy, his eyes searching. Julia was there, three paces away, her body crushed and obscured, except for a slender arm in a festive sleeve of lavender.

★   ★   ★

Simeon no longer enters the sea. He watches it now, two years later, from the shore or from the splintered fishing boat that takes him out on the odd day when there is a respite from his job and from caring for Isaac, who will soon have an artificial leg but has not yet managed to talk, or even laugh. Nina cares for him, too, but she must also tend to their six-month-old daughter, and to her piecework sewing.

Sometimes Simeon stops his car on the road above the Dingli Cliffs. He stands and looks down at the spray jetting up from the boulders hundreds of feet below, and stares over the cresting waves at the distant rock faces of Filfla. The air at the top of the cliffs whips erratically, and Simeon instinctively braces his legs against the heavy gusts. Each time he stands there, he knows that in a single unguarded moment, he could be taken. Each time, he looks out to the blue rim of the sea and relaxes his body and is sharply buffeted as he thinks of that day, but he is not lifted away.

A QUESTION OF THE TIDE

I say Romero should've taken a lesson from the mud crabs. They're spread out by the thousands when the tide gives them leeway in the mangroves, and if a man walks among them in the slop, all the crabs inside a four-step radius dodge into their holes. You take another step, and the next circle scats and dives. They're out again as soon as you pass, swiveling those eyes on little stalks. Wary. Smart.

This guy Romero was chatty but only in spurts, so he left me wondering if we really were chums after all. Both of us were up from Buenos Aires, *porteños* just scraping by and all that. Even solitary surfers chunk-up when they're dipping new breaks, especially in a far-gone place like this, way up from Bahia, so that's what we were doing, hanging together, getting by on Spanish even though the locals speak Portuguese. And I tell you this: what they say about Spanish and Portuguese being born of the same mother—well, one of them is a bastard. The body language is a whole other story. Romero could vouch for that.

When he did talk, Romero loved to spout off about beautiful nature this, beautiful nature that, going on and on about the little fish that swam just in front of his nose for a whole hour in the maze of the reef that shelters this stretch of coast. No normal wave raker goes in for that sentimental stuff. We've got one thing on the brain. Not Romero, and he paid for it.

It all started when he had to chuck the board a few days after we met, when I clipped him on a niner tube I didn't want to share. Greedy bastard, that's me, and famous for it. Maybe that's why only a Romero could put up with yours truly. But shit, I didn't mean for him to take that rip on the reef. A better man would've slapped shallow. He didn't. Probably daydreaming about the guppy on his nose. So Mister Hairy Reef took a chomp on Romero's chest. I helped him back to the sand, blood screaming out. Some old nurse, maybe just a seamstress, sewed him up, and the color came back to Romero's face. Never said a bitchy word about it. Problem was, the bite was on the ribs that met the board when he paddled. So oops, no more surfing this trip.

Believe this? He said he'd pay for chow at a shack on the beach that night. I wondered if he was going to sprinkle cyanide on my crab when I went for a pee, but when I came back he was talking to a big man and his woman who'd sat at our little table. Big Guy, called Sergio, was freckly white, could've been one of those Irish rugby players you see on TV. His babe was brown and slim—looked Italian to me, but turns out they were both natives. That's Brazil. They kissed while we cracked the crabs and shoveled bits of octopus.

The waitress wasn't much, so I kept my eyes on Marisa, Sergio's wife or who-knows-what, trying to catch a look. No go. But the way Romero told it, even while Sergio and Marisa were lip to lip, Marisa was pressing her bare feet against Romero's in the sand. Even poking her toes in the gaps between his. I would've thought that was an invitation for a threesome, but Sergio didn't seem to be in on the party. Romero's not bad looking, sure, but Marisa could've poked her little piggies my way. Now I'm glad she didn't.

They made Romero show his wound with all the stitches. Big deal. Marisa even touched and tickled the scabby edges of the slice, both sides. Romero broke another crab and asked Sergio to tell us about the spear-fishing. Sergio was a bragger. Had such-and-such kind of double-outboard fiberglass skiff with this-and-that gear like we're supposed to care, and the precious boat was hidden in a secret spot up the estuary where only he could find it—better there than at the dock where the village lackeys would steal it. Then he got on about all the fish he'd speared two days before, sizes and types and how they fought. While he's showing his perfect aim like he's going to shoot the waitress over at the grill, I see Marisa's hand go beneath the table and I'm sure it was on Romero's leg or worse because Romero dropped a pink claw and gave some attention to Sergio's aim. But I could swear that a second later that bastard Romero had shifted in his chair to get a little closer to Marisa. Might've been rubbing his knee against hers; who knows? All I can say is, I started concentrating on which way Sergio's eyes were pointed too. Just when he turned back from the imaginary hunt, I knocked the table leg with my heel. Two beers went down, one gushing onto Sergio's lap. He didn't seem to catch what was going on, only started singing some tune about spilled beer and the romance that always followed and wrapped Marisa in his big arms until she seemed to disappear. Sergio ended up paying the whole tab; said he liked surfers and hoped he could learn to hit the waves himself someday.

The way Romero told it, next day he bumped into Marisa and Sergio on the beach road. Sergio stopped his black pickup truck and asked if Romero needed a ride to town. Marisa opened the door and let her leg dangle out. Romero said no thanks, he'd hoof it, take in the nature. Nature, sure—Marisa's lean leg for instance, that's what I'da been thinking. But Sergio took him at his word and said he and Romero should go fishing the next day since the wound meant his surfing was busted. He said there was lots of *nature* in the blue at the far edge of the reef, and that no doubt Romero was a fucking good swimmer, and the season was right, and he's got two spearguns, he needs to give the outboards a run anyway to keep them healthy, and the tide will be up just after breakfast. Helluva pitch from Sergio—damn well thought out, if you ask me. And I wonder if Romero was interested because he thought Marisa would be fishing too. I gotta be honest here: Marisa was tasty to the eye. If she'd put her sandy toes on mine, I'd be in the same fix.

Anyway, Romero agrees to go fishing.

Morning. There was action where the reef makes an underwater point before it gives way to the river mouth. I barely said a hey-yah to Romero while I was humping it toward the beach. I looked back when I was paddling out. Saw him get into that black truck. No sign of Marisa.

The way Romero told it, Sergio was all friendly and eager when they were slogging around trying to find his boat. Wasn't easy. Up this stream and the next, knee-deep in mangrove muck until they found the secret spot. Then a prop got stuck in the mud. At least he was right about the tide. They got out of the estuary and headed toward what Sergio called big game country. Big game? Why Romero didn't just dive overboard and swim back to an easy beach and easier pleasures, I don't know, and it bugs me, just like that amused look he always had on his face, as if he was in on some funny secret and there was no way he was going to share it.

First business on the boat was learning how to shoot the spear. How to cock the long rubber band, the maximum distance for a hit. Child's play, but Sergio made a big deal out of it. He said he was always proud to bring a big fish back to Marisa for dinner. She couldn't cook, but a chef in the village would make it just the way she liked it, and Marisa deserved a good fish. Always.

They put on masks and jumped in. Telling this, I'm prickly. Romero in the water with an armed man whose girlfriend has been feeling Romero up. Sure, Romero's got a speargun too. But who knows where Sergio is coming from? Rather take my chances with the sharks, and there are plenty of them here by the reef. Adds a little juice to the surfing, makes you want to hang topside as far as the wave can take you.

Water's a little murky. Sergio is ahead. He looks back at Romero and points down. They both dive. Sergio with that big chest—I bet he could take a nap on the bottom before he'd need air. They dove a few times, missed on two shots, and reloaded at the surface. Out of the blue, Sergio says his gal is hot, right? Romero thinks about this, then says everybody's got their own thing. Sergio says you mean she's *not* hot?

Right here I'm thinking of that species of woman who tries to seduce you, and if you don't join in she'll tell her man you've tried to get between her legs and you're fucked either way. But this being the southern hemisphere, it's all upside down, and it's the man who's trying to trip you up.

Romero spiels it like a diplomat, says that all Brazilian women are hot, that's why everyone comes to Brazil. So she's *hot, right*? Sergio says again. Romero admits it: Marisa is fucking hot. What do you mean *fucking* hot? I mean, you're a lucky man, Romero says. Sergio isn't satisfied with lucky. Think I got her by luck? I worked on her since she was fourteen. Made her have my bed. A virgin. Call that luck? Call that *luck*?

Two guys bobbing up and down, treading and talking like this—the water can be rough outside the reef. You pump your legs and sweep your one free arm to keep your mouth above the waves. And Romero's got to think fast at the same time, poor sucker.

You call that luck? Sergio wants an answer. I have *bad* luck, says Romero. Probably thinks he's pulling a rabbit out of a hat with this one: he says the cut on his chest is bleeding again. Time to go back to the boat.

Sergio says, don't worry, he'll shoot any shark that comes, and thanks for being the bait. He looks down through his mask at the strings of blood coming from Romero's chest and says this is real hunting. Never

speared a shark before. Marisa will love eating it with
moqueca sauce.

The way Romero told it, Sergio meant what he said
about the shark hunting—kept himself between Romero
and the boat, with the speargun not aimed at Romero,
but not too far off target either. Come on, the hunt's
just beginning, says Sergio, give it a little time; I won't
let them chew on you. We're fishing buddies. And I'm
a damn good shot.

Romero's cut is wide open and leaking more. I'd seen
it when he got clipped, and it was deep like a hatchet
had landed there. He'd just pressed a hand on it till we
found the seamstress. Tough guy for a nature lover.

Romero tries to angle off, wide of the reef, toward
the river mouth, thinks he'll just skip the boat and swim
back. But Sergio swims with him, and now they're doing
water ballet right where the grays like to feast—where
the fresh water meets the salty sea.

Sergio keeps up his buddy-buddy talk, says they'll
be heroes in the village when he and Romero motor in
with a shark and pull it up on the dock. And then he
says....He's shouting over the rocking water when he
says: Marisa will *love* us if we get this shark. She'll *love* us.

★   ★   ★

Romero sort of lost track of things after that—his memory of the whole thing is full of potholes. Next thing he recalls is dragging Sergio across the mangrove mud with the crabs running to their tunnels. Sergio's left arm was missing, but Romero'd managed to squeeze the stump with the diced-up rubber band from Sergio's speargun before he pulled the big guy through the rooty tangle.

Here's where I come in. Sergio is lying in the little clinic. The shark had laid some teeth into his hip, too, but I guess it hadn't been big enough to make him a meal. Arm gone, hip chewed, some scrapes to the face. Bunch of village folks are huddled around, saying last month's case was worse. Romero is there, muddy pile on the floor.

Sergio is in and out of it, eyes every which way. Marisa struts in. Sergio comes to. He starts howling and wailing and telling her how much he loves her, begging to know if she feels the same. Begging and begging. Marisa puts a hand on his face and strokes his mucky hair. Shush, shush, she says. You're a strong man, a real man. You'll be all right. Sergio tries to reach for her with his one arm but he's too weak. You love me? He goes on with the begging. You love me? You love me? All she says is let them put the bandages on and I'll drive you to the big hospital. Then I'll take you home. She keeps stroking him and stroking him. Never looks at Romero and me. I'm happy for that.

I pull Romero up to his feet. I'm thinking Sergio and his woman are lost somewhere in the tidal zone on a shore break—high tide is love, low tide is hate. Maybe vice versa. Between them is where you can get the best ride, if the swell is strong and the wind is right and....Hell, what am I talking about? Love? Me?

Outside the clinic door it's too bright, and Romero feels too heavy on my shoulder, like he's passing out. But then, when I've sat him down to drink a squeeze of *maracujá* at a street stall, Romero perks up. He tells me Sergio saved his life. Shot the shark just in time, then the thing turned on Sergio. Romero wants to go back and tell that to Marisa.

Saved his life! I laugh. Romero tries to get up, but I shove him back down, and it's a good thing he's still too beat because I'll tackle him if he tries to go back there. Saved your life? I say. I pull off my T-shirt and wad it up, press it against the weepy reef bite on his chest. And while I'm handing him more juice, I'm thinking Romero shouldn't have let me steal that niner tube, shouldn't have been daydreaming about the guppy on his nose, shouldn't have gone fishing, and I'm telling myself it's all his fault.

BORDER CONTROL

Gerrit was already griping to himself about the icy darkness he was rolling toward, his truck loaded with flowers, of all things. They'd been flown in from Bolivia and stacked in his trailer for the three-day haul from his Rotterdam base to Moscow, where somebody would cough up the money to buy them. Gerrit couldn't see how it all added up, delicate flowers traveling so far across the surface of the earth, but maybe the dark and forlorn Russian winter made such things of beauty even more valuable.

As he passed from Holland into Germany he slid The Doors into the CD player to help him through the long hours of highway creep before he would hit Poland, where the road would break open again—less crowded, bumpier, and lined with ragged fields. Alenka, his girl-friend, had finally started to warm up to The Doors on Gerrit's last run through Tallinn in Estonia, where she lived. But she still found it strange that a guy her own age, twenty-five, loved such ancient music. She was Russian, she said, but born and raised there in Estonia. How she could call herself Russian when she'd been born in a different country where she'd lived all of her life—it was the seed of just one of their many arguments. They saw each other for no more than three days at a stretch in Tallinn and either fought or fornicated the whole time, even when they were eating. It was easy in the cab of his truck. A bed was wedged behind the seats, and he could pull a portable gas stove out of the wide dashboard. In the tight space of the cab he hit her sometimes, and sometimes he regretted it.

Alenka the witch, Alenka the itch. Hours later, as he rumbled through Poland's midsection, he still hadn't shaken her out of his mind. If it hadn't been for the customs fiasco that almost landed him in jail, he wouldn't have met her. Fertilized chicken eggs had taken him to Tallinn that time, incubating in the warmth from the trailer's heater as they formed little hearts and bones and beaks. He had imagined seeing them inside their shells, sprouting organs from nowhere. One million four hundred twenty thousand incubating baby birds. Why had he worried about them cooling off and dying when they were just going to get chopped up a few weeks later anyway? "Desperate for company," was all he could answer to himself. When he arrived in Tallinn, the customs agent found a cache of high-end stereos behind the egg crates, which Gerrit swore he knew nothing about. It took five days and plenty of bills for the Estonian authorities to sort it out, and it was during that time that he'd met Alenka, one of a clutch of girls he'd glued himself to in a basement pub.

The truck barreled on, through the elongating tunnel made by its headlights in the frigid night of eastern Poland. Gerrit scoffed to himself about how absurd it was that people would live and could live in winter lands like these that were perpetually gray and, even worse, had only a few hours of daytime somewhere there above the blanket of clouds.

When he was beyond the Polish border, with twelve more hours to Moscow, he pulled over at one of the overnight stations to get some sleep among the other rigs huddled together like vulnerable sheep. Here in Belarus and in Russia, even with other trucks around, when Gerrit took a piss he did it from his driver's seat out the open door, instead of standing out there in the frozen mud. Another driver had told him of standing for a pee on the route outside Petersburg when he'd felt a pistol barrel jabbing his neck. "While I've got both my hands busy with the big gun down below!" he had joked. But the driver had lost his truck to the hijackers. Gerrit threw an extra blanket on his bed, set the engine to run all night at a low idle, and got his sleep.

The next day it all went without a fight—the border check near Smolensk, the short spat over his transporter's visa, the timid stalling of the customs weasels, the tedious unloading—it all went smoothly because they all knew who owned the flower trade. The depot outside of Moscow was a maze of concrete warehouses, loading docks, and crowded trailers on a tract of cracked asphalt and blackened snow. After the unloading and the obligatory round of jollies with the bull-shaped men who controlled the paperwork, Gerrit got paid in cash. He was eager to stash it and get on. Snowflakes as big as thumbprints were starting to fall.

He walked through the corridors between trailers back to his truck, leery of all the blind corners. He pulled out his keys.

"*Misss-ter!*" The voice sounded like a hissing snake. It came from somewhere near the ground. Gerrit jerked his head around and scanned the underbellies of the surrounding trailers. He saw only a small plume of vapor coming from behind a double set of wheels on the rig next to his own. Gerrit swung his eyes in a full circle, worried he was being set up by a team. He wedged his key into the frozen lock.

"*Misss-ter!* I pay you!"

Gerrit turned around slowly, like a bear on hind legs, sniffing. This time a hooded head and an oversized green coat emerged from behind the black tires. *It's a goddamn Chinese*, thought Gerrit.

"*Misss-ter!* Put me in your truck. Take me to next place after Germany. I give you eight thousands German mark halfway. Eight more when I am there."

Gerrit's eyes caught those on the nearly hidden face, then he turned his head, pulled the key out of the lock, and started to walk toward the alley formed by the two trucks ahead of his. He whirled around when he heard a quick mashing of footsteps; the Chinese couldn't stop before slamming into Gerrit. Gerrit shoved hard and the green coat went down. A hand poked out from it, clutching a thick wad of marks.

"Please! I give you cash. Take me!"

"Shut up." Gerrit's voice was low. "Shut up and follow me. Behind me." After several paces, he turned.

It was a woman's face under the hood, almost a girl's. If it hadn't been, he would have grabbed the steel pipe he kept in his cab and chased away the bulky green coat. Instead, he motioned for her to come around to the front of his truck, in the narrow gap between it and the next trailer, to keep her out of view.

"You speak English?"

"Yes I can, speak English. I going to Europe. To Engaland. Or Brussels. You take me."

"If you make any trouble, I'll throw you on the road and keep the money. Those are the rules for roaches like you. Let me see it."

She squinted and thrust the wad toward him, gripping the half-payment with both hands. He glanced at it, took it, then brusquely patted his gloved hands all over the lumpy coat, searching for anything hard and lethal. Her petite body resisted the pressure of his hands with a strength that surprised him.

"And if they catch you, I don't know you. You're just a roach. A friend of mine is locked up thanks to roaches like you. Get in and climb up to the top bunk. When we're out of here on the road, you have to go in the back, in the trailer."

The top bed was a metal frame with a crossweave of elastic bands; it folded down from the wall, and once the girl was in it, he pushed it partway back up. It looked like it held no more than a stray sleeping bag.

She said nothing. The truck crept through the maze of the depot yard and emerged from the barbed wire gates onto a road whose icy glaze was quickly collecting a snowy coat. The girl stayed tucked away above Gerrit. He wanted to be well clear of the city before letting her down.

"Why do you speak English?" Gerrit's voice boomed in the privacy of the cab.

"I studied in school."

"Huh. A smarty Chinese on the rough road to riches." She didn't answer; Gerrit read it as shrewdness. "You're betting a stack of money that you'll win big in England or somewhere. If you don't get killed on the way. What's wrong with China, anyway? No room left?"

"No work and no money."

"No money? That's a bunch of marks you have. Enough to buy a car."

"People borrow it to me."

Gerrit braked lightly as a truck in front of him recovered from a skid. He could see that it was going to be an ugly night of rutted snow and cigarettes, and he decided it was a better idea in this weather not to stop to toss her in the trailer; he'd figure something out before the Estonian border. If she made it as far as Tallinn with him, the girl would have to find her own good times while Gerrit was busy with Alenka.

"What about boyfriends? Any boyfriend?" Gerrit heard only a muffled breath from above. Then she spoke.

"Why do you drive a truck?"

"Because I can make good money. I like being on the road." He sucked deeply on a cigarette.

"Your father drive a truck?"

"My father? Yeah, he's always been driving. Can't stay home more than a week without a big fight with my mama."

"That why you drive a truck."

Her tone was so steady and matter-of-fact that Gerrit decided there wasn't an insult in what she said. He shoved his hand into a bin beneath his seat to pull out a candy bar. As soon as he stretched his arm upward, she plucked it from his fingers. She bit into it quickly.

"You sure make enough noise when you eat."

The girl kept chewing. Headlights from a string of a dozen trucks were in Gerrit's eyes; he squinted as they trundled past, leaving him to adjust again to the darkness of the road.

"So you are Chinese but you want to live in England. Will you still be Chinese when you live there?"

"What kind of question? I am Chinese. Chinese always."

"And what do your mama and papa think about you jumping into trucks?"

"Father love Falun Dafa, Falun Gong." She was still smacking at the candy bar. "You know them? Crazy. Crazy sit like that and move strange. Police take him. My mother not so stupid. She not likes Falun Dafa. She look for him. But she not so sad. Maybe he dead. Father and Mother, not so close. Maybe she...is happy now."

"You mean that sect."

"So crazy, those people. Even they know government come get them. Maybe kill them."

"So, Mr. China took your father, maybe killed him, and you are proud to be Chinese. Maybe if they kill your mother, too, you will be Chinese Chinese. Extra Chinese." Gerrit glanced into the rearview mirror, trying to catch a glimpse of her face, but he only saw the metal frame of the hanging bed as it reflected the lights of another passing truck.

"I be Chinese till I die. Look at me. Chinese."

"When I look at you, you could be Japanese. Or Korean. Or Mongolian, I don't know. You think your face makes you something?"

"China is great country. Great history." The girl paused. "What are you?"

"Sure, great history. Mao killing all those Chinese peasants. Starving them to death."

"You politic man? What are you? What country?" She leaned over the metal rim of the bunk and looked down at him.

"I am Dutch. Holland. Great trading nation." Gerrit laughed.

"You are white."

Gerrit dragged on a cigarette and stared at the straight and empty road. "I am white plus extra. A grandmother from Indonesia. She looked Chinese to me in the pictures. I never met her. Her name sounded Chinese. Something like Wang," said Gerrit.

"You are lucky if you part Chinese."

"Woo-ha! So lucky. I'll go take your place in China. Can your mother cook? Kung Pao chicken. I like that."

"You too big. Eat too much. More Snickers. You have some?"

"Hah! Who eats too much?" Gerrit reached into his bin and handed another snack up to her. He tried to snare her fingers in his, but she avoided it, snatching away the candy bar.

"I pay you. Cash. No funny business." She peeled away the wrapper.

"But we same race. Make good Chinese babies," Gerrit replied. He chuckled, but he stopped abruptly when he heard a scraping sound above him, from the roof of the cab. Maybe it was just a shard of hardened snow sliding off.

"Did you hear that?"

"All I hear is the truck and bad music. You have *Titanic*?"

"For a roach you sure are pushy."

"*Roadge*. What is that?"

"An ugly bug. Crawls around everywhere where people live."

"I am ugly?"

"I don't even know what you look like under that army coat. But a roach is not all bad. It survives. When all the humans have cooked themselves with nukes, the roaches will still be there, helping themselves to the kitchens."

Gerrit tensed his hands on the wheel. He'd heard the sound again, above his head. He surveyed the snow-laden track spanning ahead of his headlights, searching for enough of a shoulder to pull over.

"We're going to stop."

36

He pressed the brakes lightly at first, then strongly. The behemoth machine jolted as it hit the mounds of snow and ice along the edge of the highway. There were no other vehicles behind or ahead. The road was like a small canyon, with walls of black forest. The truck finally stopped, throwing light forward into the chasm; the red of the rear lights was absorbed by the heavy branches of the pine trees funneling away into darkness.

Gerrit clamped the brake, opened the door, and stood on the edge of the cab, gripping the vertical bar mounted outside. He reached up with one arm and placed it on the roof, feeling with his bare hand. He heard a rustling sound. Gerrit stifled a curse and crouched back into the cab to pull out the steel pipe from beneath his seat. He heard the rustling sound again. A chunk of snow fell outside the open door.

"What the problem?"

"Shut up."

Gerrit rose again outside the cab and slammed the pipe across the top, hitting the airfoil. He swung again and hit something soft. There was another sound, a frantic scraping. Gerrit swung again and again, jumping up from the sill of the doorway with every blow. There was a yelp at last.

A beam of headlights approached, and Gerrit retreated into the cab. A van passed without slowing. He pulled himself out of the cab again and reached higher with the pipe, slamming it down with wide arcs of his long arm. Then there were shouts. Gerrit put his foot on a metal step and pressed his leg to rise above the roof, his pipe raised. He could barely make out a huddled mass, which he beat again. Legs extended from the lump and it slid off the opposite side of the cab.

Gerrit pulled himself back into the truck and slammed the door. He jammed the gearshift and thrust his foot against the throttle pedal. The truck lurched, then faltered, its headlights dimming momentarily; Gerrit had to put the hiccupping engine back in neutral. A small upright body appeared in the glare of the headlights. It scrambled through the chunks of snow around to the driver's door, where the orange running lights illuminated a face below the window. Gerrit revved the engine again as he pressed his foot against the clutch.

"Stop. I know him. Stop!" The girl reached down and grabbed Gerrit's hair.

The body outside pounded on the base of the door. Gerrit put the truck into gear, but it rumbled forward slowly, jarred by the small mountains of hardened snow.

"Stop!" the voice above him barked again. "I know him. He my brother!"

"Your brother, hah. This is no bus. No one's going to use *me*!" Gerrit revved the engine and the truck ground slowly through the mounds of ice.

The bundled body outside ran alongside the truck, banging a hand on the fender. Then it ran ahead, with its hooded head tucked down, and appeared in the headlights ten yards beyond the slowly accelerating truck-beast. The bundle stood there with its arms hanging down and a pair of eyes staring at Gerrit's windshield.

The girl swung down from the bunk as if it were a trapeze, pulling at Gerrit's right arm. "Stop! His name is Wang Li! My brother!"

Gerrit's foot released the throttle pedal, but it was too late. There was a dull thump as he jammed his foot on the brake. The girl screamed.

"I'll shoot all you roaches!" Gerrit hit her again and shoved his door open. He reached beneath the seat to grab his pistol. "Brother. Hah. Brother you leave to freeze up there." The girl was silent.

A piercing cold gust hit Gerrit as he jumped down into the snow, the pipe in his hand. He had to shield his eyes from the glare of the headlights to make out the mound with legs sticking out at odd angles. The legs moved. It pulled its knees beneath it and its torso rose. The bulky green coat looked the same as the girl's. Gerrit raised the pipe and slugged it sideways against the coat. The torso fell, leaving the face upturned. It spoke. The words were unintelligible. It gasped for breath. The vapor came out of its mouth in little puffs made white by the headlights.

Gerrit reached down and pulled up on the hood of the coat. The legs planted themselves. There was snot running down from the nose. Gerrit yelled at it in Dutch, then in English.

"You fuckin' little animal! Use me? Trying to use me?"

He patted it down the same way he had done to the girl, but this one wobbled with every slap of his hand, and Gerrit had to keep it standing by holding on to its hood. It cried out when Gerrit's hand hit its chest.

"You little bugger. All you got is a busted rib or two." Gerrit jerked the coat again, but before he could slam the head into the engine grille, the girl flung herself into the back of Gerrit's legs. His knees folded and he toppled over as the girl screamed in Chinese and scrambled onto the injured young man, who had crumpled with Gerrit's fall.

Gerrit dragged himself away, his bare hands raking razors of ice, then stumbled to his feet and pulled out the pistol. He pointed it at the pile of two people, his chest heaving. Gerrit thought they suddenly looked very small. He shifted the muzzle upward and fired. The shot hit the ice not far from the girl's head. She screamed and crawled to Gerrit's feet and pounded his legs with her fists.

"My brother! My brother!"

Gerrit kicked her with his left foot, then his right, then his left again. He put a foot on her back and stepped on it, then walked around to the door of the cab and hoisted himself up. He put his face into the triangle between the open door and the windshield. "Get out of the way or I'll drive over you."

"Our name is Wang, like you! My brother is hurt. You so rich, white man."

"You can fucking sleep here with your boyfriend, forever."

"No boyfriend. Little brother. Little brother."

The girl ran to the door and climbed up to grab one of Gerrit's ankles. He shook his leg, trying to free himself of her.

"You make us die here? You murder us?" She slipped and her chin banged against the steel step, but she kept her clasp on Gerrit's ankle and remained dangling above the ground.

A glint of light caught Gerrit's attention as he glared down at her. It was far away, but in a moment it divided into two little white eyes.

"Get in. Quick! Get him in too."

Gerrit switched off the headlights. The girl stumbled to the front and groped for the injured youth, lifting him to his feet and hauling him to the cab.

"Up to the bed. Now."

The girl pulled the groaning body and Gerrit pushed it upward. Gerrit slammed the door shut as the approaching truck slowed down. He lit a cigarette and turned up the CD player. The truck slowed to a creep as it neared. Gerrit's eyes met those of the other driver, who veered close and stopped an arm's length away. The driver had fleshy jowls that barely moved as he spoke, in Russian. Gerrit shrugged and flicked cigarette ashes, saying "I'm okay, just resting." The driver looked into the cab, his eyeballs catching the orange color of the running lights as he probed with his stare.

"Bad night for the road." Gerrit half-smiled. "Time for a smoke."

The driver raised two fingers to his mouth as if they held a cigarette. Gerrit reached for the pack on the dashboard and held it out the window. The driver took it with a mitt of a hand and grunted. Gerrit waved at him to keep the pack and took a long drag on his cigarette. The other truck's engine roared and the gears caught. The hulk rumbled away into the darkness.

Gerrit switched off the music and set his own truck rolling. The labored breathing coming from above was occasionally audible over the mechanical crescendo as the truck gained speed.

"Thank you."

Gerrit's grip was hard on the wheel. "Thank you for what? Beating your brother? Stepping on you?" There was no answer, only the soft growling of the truck. He lit another cigarette. "You can thank me when I dump you both at the next stop. How is he?"

There was a staccato exchange of Chinese above Gerrit's head.

"He hurt."

Gerrit grunted and fumbled for a candy bar. "Can he eat?"

She took the raised sweet. Gerrit heard the wrapper snap open. He lifted up a bottle of water as well. The snow was falling heavily. The truck and the three travelers slid by a half-dozen dimly lit towns in the night. Two hours passed before she spoke.

"You want more money."

Gerrit didn't answer.

"I give you more money. For my brother."

"The brother you put on top to freeze to death?"

"I don't know he on top."

"Hah! And my mother is a virgin." Gerrit exploded in angry laughter. The truck swerved briefly, swiping a snowbank before he brought it back straight.

"I don't know he on top. I go away from him. Where the trucks, all the trucks. Okay, not my brother. My cousin. But same as brother."

"So with a hundred trucks you both ended up with me. By luck. What luck! I almost shot you. Yeah, you are lucky."

"I pay you more."

Gerrit loaded his Brazilian music and started singing to it, as best he could. When it was over he thought

43

about Alenka in Tallinn, the next stop, where he'd take on a load of fish and screw her in the cab for one night, maybe two, depending on how much he would have to pay the depot operators for the extra parking time. There was one fuel stop between here and Estonia. And then the border control. Sometimes they inspected, even at night.

"How much?" he said. "I come from a great trading nation. Great history." Gerrit tried to catch a glimpse of her through the rearview mirror.

"Engaland. I give you two times money."

"I'm not going to England. I will drop you in Germany, after going down from Tallinn."

"Tow win. What is that?"

"The next stop after fueling up, in a few hours. I will stop there for a night. Then to Germany. Germany is very good for Chinese."

Gerrit wanted to return her deceit with some of his own. At Tallinn he would load up and drive onto a ferry that would take him and the fish to Kiel in Germany, but he would shake off the freeloaders in Tallinn, well before the port inspectors would find them. He'd be doing the two roaches a favor, saving them from being captured and jailed or deported. And she wouldn't have to pay the second half. But he had to shake them off before Alenka showed up.

44

The windshield wipers were scraping off the plastering snow, barely keeping up, as the truck approached the fuel stop—a slushy line of rigs casting shadows beneath sparse fluorescent lights suspended from aluminum wings. Gerrit told his passengers they'd have to squeeze tighter so he could push up the hinged bunk as far as possible.

When the tanks were full, Gerrit pulled ahead to a wide space beyond the pumps to quickly check the tires and knock the ice out of the wheel wells with his pipe. As he banged the last set of wheels, just behind the cab on the left side, his flashlight caught a piece of ice-caked fabric hanging like a rag. Gerrit looked back at the glow around the pumps to be sure no one was watching. He went down on his knees and saw what looked like a gunnysack wedged between the axle and the chassis above it. There was a cord wrapped around the icy sack, securing it to the axle and the brake lines running near it. His light shone upon two legs strapped to the axle struts. Gerrit could see that the fabric of the sack was partly torn away and had been caught in the joint between the axle and the wheel. He reached up and pushed his fist against the sack. It didn't move. A truck leaving the pumps approached and flashed its headlights. Gerrit stood up and waved at it with a thumbs-up. The passing truck gnashed into a higher gear and Gerrit jumped into his cab.

"Fuck you. You have a fucking big family."

"What?"

"Shut up."

Gerrit started up the truck and rolled onto the road. After half an hour at the highest speed he could manage, he veered to the shoulder and yanked the brake, yelling at the girl to get out. She tumbled down and Gerrit pulled her along, pushed her down, and shoved her head behind the trailer's front wheels. He pointed the flashlight at the body strapped to the undercarriage.

"Another brother?" The girl struggled beneath Gerrit's grip. "Look! Another cousin? Another cousin you leave to die?"

Gerrit pulled on her coat, ramming her head against the steel chassis, then he let go of her. He crawled behind the tires and pulled out a switchblade. He cut the cords.

"Now, you. You pull it down."

The girl resisted. Gerrit shook her in the crowded space beneath the rig, the flashlight beam dancing crazily with his movement. She put a hand to the bundle of gray fabric and pulled. It fell down like a log, but the part with the head remained partially suspended by the wheel-trapped fabric. Gerrit cut through the fabric with his knife and the head fell.

"You know him too?"

"No. He is dead."

"How do you know he's dead?"

With one hand Gerrit dragged the body halfway out from under the trailer. He pointed the flashlight at the Chinese face and pressed two fingers against an artery. Faint plumes of frozen breath came out of the mouth. The eyes were closed.

"You see? He's not dead." Gerrit swiveled the head, trying to wake it up.

"Almost dead." The girl crawled away and stood up. "We go now." She looked up and down the empty and lightless road, hands in her coat pockets.

Gerrit stayed on his hands and knees in the snow, thinking. The flashlight under his palm shone down the length of the body. Gerrit rose and pointed the light at the girl.

"Yes. We leave him. We leave him with your brother."

"No."

"Get your brother. Get him out."

"No."

Gerrit pulled the gun out of his vest and let it hang at his side.

"Okay, you kill me." She leaned backward against the open door, hands still in her pockets. Her face in the bright light was motionless except for the twitching of her eyelids against the sharpness of the light beam. For an instant Gerrit thought she was beautiful.

"Get him down." He stepped toward her and grabbed her wrist, pushing her toward the step up to the cab. Her arm was strong and she twisted it away from his hand, but she vaulted into the seat anyway.

Gerrit saw the pipe in her hand a moment too late. She jabbed it into his temple, stunning him. He fell backward onto the road. The door banged shut. The engine had been left running and now it began to scream. Gerrit could hear the transmission grinding as he struggled to get up from the packed ruts of snow. The truck heaved forward and stopped, the engine choking. It pounced again, then it halted. If it had gone a yard further, the rear wheels would have crushed the frozen man lying beneath the trailer.

Gerrit got up and opened the door, pointing the gun at her. He reached beyond the wheel and switched off the ignition. He could feel his temple swelling up and throbbing, but a calmness had come over him.

"You can stop now. Get him down. We'll put them in the back together. Give me the pipe."

She handed it to him slowly, speaking tersely in Chinese, first toward Gerrit and then upward toward her compatriot. Gerrit kept his distance as she helped the injured young man out of the bunk and walked him to the back of the trailer. Once the young man was lying in the empty bay, Gerrit made the girl drag the other freeloader to the rear, and together they hoisted the groaning, stiff body over the metal cusp and laid him next to the cousin.

"It's cold back here. Tie them together. They'll keep each other warm." He meant it, for their survival. And he meant it as a test, a punishment for her. Gerrit stepped forward into the bay to pick up two rolls of canvas straps. He handed them to the girl.

"Around their chests and their legs. Arms too. Together. Close."

The cousin tried to twist away as the girl followed instructions, but Gerrit pinned him with his knee while keeping the gun on the girl. She put the straps around the two young men, back to back.

"Make it tighter. Put another around them."

The girl snarled but did not speak. She did what he said.

"Now we'll get blankets."

Gerrit let her jump down from the bay first; he followed her, the gun in one hand, the pipe in the other, and the flashlight tucked in his armpit. She pulled two thick blankets out of the cab and they walked back toward the rear.

"Maybe that man have money," she said. "You take it. You take him. You leave us here. We go back to the other trucks."

Gerrit stopped in midstep. He thought of the distance back to the fuel stop and whether the man with the broken ribs could make it.

"That's a good idea. So you can freeze too. Like your cousin and the man on the axle."

The girl looked at the gun. "Maybe I stay with you, you shoot me. Better the cold. A new truck."

Gerrit thought of all the kind drivers he knew. Not a one. Not even his father. They were all men who liked the battles of the road because they relieved the monotony of the road. Men who beat their prostitutes with delight and delighted in telling their comrades about it at fuel stops. All of them older than he was, with jocular malice in their eyes. Maybe he would turn into one of them after a few more years of this. He thought of the inconvenience, maybe danger, of having the girl with him in the cab for the next few hours until they reached the border around dawn.

He watched her watching him.

Gerrit pushed her to the high open doors at the rear and told her to get in. As soon as her feet had cleared the edge of the bay, he slammed the steel doors shut. When he slid the bolt lock, he heard her shouting in Chinese. Then she shouted something in English, but he couldn't make it out because he was already stepping around to the cab. Yes, it would be cold back there. If she had sense she'd huddle with the other two under the blankets.

What a sight that would be—the girl lying next to the man, one of her tribe, that she had wanted to leave to die. She would probably untie him from her "cousin." Probably she had done it already.

Gerrit played The Doors as he drove. A trickle of blood found its way to the corner of his mouth, and he licked it instinctively before wiping it away. His temple was pulsing. For a while he faintly heard a pounding sound from behind, but then it went away. In a day or two that bay would be full of frozen fish, from top to bottom. He was dying to feel Alenka's body. He had made it with her once back there in the trailer, standing up, when it was warmer a few months earlier.

Gerrit's palms moistened as he thought of the risks at the border and the possible delays. The Estonian customs police were tougher these days. A little cash didn't go as far. And Alenka would give up on him. Alenka and her long legs.

A few hours later Gerrit slowed the truck when the border station's lights appeared in the distance. In his vibrating side mirror there was a horizon of clouded gray light. Gusts were smacking the ice-rimmed windows, but there was no snow falling. He pulled the truck onto the shoulder of the road, brushing the trees of the sparse woods. He left the engine running and the music of an Estonian acid rock group playing loudly. Alenka had given it to him, and he didn't like it.

When he released the lock bar at the rear and swung the doors open, he saw three separate lumps. Gerrit climbed into the bay with his gun ahead of him. He pushed a foot against the closest one and reached down to turn the face so he could see it. He did the same with the next nearest. He didn't need to check for a pulse or breath, but he did anyway. He saw that both their coats were unzipped. The third lump was the girl, in a fetal position under both blankets at a far front corner of the dark space. She moved groggily when he nudged her with his foot, then she started shivering and her eyes opened. He pulled her up to her feet and her shivering turned into shaking.

"They're dead. You have to get out of here. I'm sorry about your cousin. You can walk through the forest to get around the border patrol. Get to the other side. Find another truck. I'll give you your money back."

Gerrit held one of her arms to help her walk. As he led her around the two dead young men, he saw papers protruding from their unbuttoned pockets. A strong gust from the open doors pushed the girl into Gerrit's chest and scattered some of the papers. When they reached the edge of the bay, he jumped out first. She was too wobbly to make it out on her own. Gerrit lifted her down and pointed toward the forest.

"You go here, to the right, through the trees...."

"Give me my money," she said.

"Okay. I'll get it. I'm sorry about your cousin." He turned and started toward the cab to get the money. When he heard her call after him, he ignored her.

Gerrit was pulling the wad of money from the underside of the dashboard before he absorbed what she had said. *Not my cousin. I do not know him.* He switched off the banging music and stepped quickly to the rear of the trailer.

She was gone. For a split second he saw a green coat darting between the trees. Gerrit started to shout, but stopped himself. The cold air filled his open mouth.

He heaved himself up into the bay and stuffed the identification papers back into the young men's otherwise empty pockets. Their bodies were already stiff, and as he pulled them out, he held them by their armpits so their heads wouldn't crash against the ground. He dragged each one into the trees, laying them next to each other, arranging their arms and legs. He kicked snow over them, extra snow over the faces, and bent down to sweep away his footprints as he stepped backward to the truck.

Gerrit slammed the steel doors shut. He was tired, and relieved. She, too, was heartless. Brutal, and a thief. He told himself she was even more brutal than he had become. He looked over his shoulder at the two mounds. Only now that they were dead did he think of them as people. He turned and trudged to the front of the truck;

his feet were heavy and block-like in the cold, and it made walking in the deep snow difficult. Awkwardly, he climbed back into the cab and tried hard to think of Alenka as he put the idling engine into gear.

YOUR MOTHERS MUST COME

At first Tevi did not understand. "All your mothers must come to the session next Thursday," said Madame in her sharpest voice. "All your mothers. And tell them to wear tights and something tight-fitting on top. No exceptions."

Tevi heard anger every time Madame Tixier spoke, and never saw her smile. The other girls in the ballet school whispered that Madame had stopped dancing and left France because she broke her back while performing. But she didn't seem to Tevi to have a broken back. The woman was as straight as a pencil. And pointed like a pencil, thought Tevi. How Madame Tixier had ended up here in little Ramla, in Israel, none of the other girls knew, or at least Tevi had not heard them say; they usually kept their distance from Tevi, who was straight like half a pencil, and not good with words.

The class had been divided into two groups earlier in the year, and it was obvious that the girls in one group were a little fatter, or had bigger hips. Some were even beginning to look like women, with breasts that seemed enormous to Tevi, who was put into the group of skinnies, the group whose mothers were ordered to come to class in tights the following Thursday.

The trouble was that Tevi had no mother.

Madame Tixier could have known this, but she didn't. She seemed to care for nothing more than perfect leg extensions and finely arched feet and vertical spines and arms that floated. She didn't even know the girls' names. So Madame simply didn't know—or perhaps she had devised a special form of torture, thought Tevi.

The Thursday of the Mothers was preceded by a week of daily training that left Tevi with soreness in her legs every night, especially in the muscles that ran like rubber bands along the backs of her thighs. Tevi didn't mind the hard exercises, and she didn't mind Madame's snapping criticisms. Sometimes, on purpose, Tevi didn't fully reach her fingers beyond her toes at the bar, to be sure to receive a correction from Madame. And occasionally, though she knew the position perfectly, she would bend a knee ever so slightly to provoke Madame's fierce glare. "You! You are not my pupil if you show such a lack of grace! You forget all you know in an instant. Point now!" And Tevi would point with legs as straight as bamboo as she looked in the mirror to see Madame's harsh regard.

On Thursday the mothers filed in, daughters at their sides. Tevi hid behind the thin wall of the entryway, where street shoes and tote bags were piled up. Then she peeked around the edge of the wall.

Madame told the mothers to stand in rows on the polished wooden floor; she walked among them, looking each mother up and down, telling them to let go of their daughters' hands and stand straight. Tevi was afraid that Madame would have some list of students in her hands, like the teachers in the morning school for reading and math, checking off who was there. But there was no list. There was only Madame, with her unblinking gaze as she told the mothers to turn around.

"Now the mothers will lie down, on their backs," said Madame in a voice so commanding that Tevi herself started to lie down in her little hiding place, but she caught herself and stood upright again. Tevi heard murmurs from several of the mothers, as if they were complaining, and she tried hard to understand what they were saying. As the murmurs subsided Tevi peered around the corner of the wall, fearful that Madame would catch a glimpse of her.

Madame stood with straight legs next to each woman in turn and bent forward from the waist, dropping her torso so low that she could reach out and pass a hand along the space between each woman's back and the floor. There was no "hmm" or "aha" from her as she made her judgments of each mother's form; the room was silent except for the breathing of the mothers and the nervous shuffling of their bewildered girls. The women lying quietly on the shiny wood floor, all in orderly rows, looked to Tevi like fruits in the market. They had such different shapes and colors and sizes, as if pears and bananas and celery and eggplants had been carefully placed in the same wooden crate.

Madame made another circuit around the room, sometimes looking directly at a mother and daughter and sometimes looking into the mirrored walls to make her survey. She tipped her head back as she circled, her lean limbs so light that she seemed not to need the floor. Tevi saw her rise on her slippered toes once or twice as she passed row by row. From time to time it seemed to Tevi that Madame was looking at herself in the wide mirror, and once she even lifted an arm into a delicate line that looked to Tevi like a tulip stem. At the end of the stem her hand took the shape of a bloom opening up, but only for an instant.

The arm fell and Madame said, "Thank you, ladies. We are done. Now it is time for class."

The women got to their feet, some rising easily, some rising awkwardly, as if they had been in bed for a long time. The whispers began, then timid exclamations. "But we didn't even get to dance," said one, whose remark was followed by laughter.

Madame said nothing more until the mothers had left, leaving their daughters in a huddle near the wall where Tevi was hiding.

"Girls, girls!" Madame announced with a clap of her thin hands. "Let us begin." Tevi slipped into the rear of the group of pupils as they started to fan out to positions across the floor.

The class that followed was unusually strenuous. Tevi did not look at Madame, not even at her image in the mirror, and she reached her legs toward the ceiling as she had never done before. She leaped and rebounded on a toe point with a lightness that surprised her. She extended her arms upward to form her own tulip stems. She ignored the pain running along her thighs, if pain even pierced her consciousness. With ease she performed the double pirouette that left the other girls askew. And all the while she never looked at Madame Tixier.

Madame clapped three times. The class was over. Tevi quickly slid to the back of the crowd of girls chatting and fiddling with their belongings behind the partition. As Tevi was reaching down to pick up a sweater, Madame's feet appeared. Tevi straightened her back but kept her gaze down; all she could see were two pairs of feet in their worn slippers. Tevi's classmates departed, but the two pairs of feet remained motionless, toe to toe.

Madame Tixier put her hand on Tevi's shoulder, just near her neck. It rested there for a moment, no heavier than a handkerchief.

"I don't need to know your mother," Madame whispered.

Then one pair of slippered feet disappeared, and Tevi was alone.

A MORNING SWIM
TO NORTH KOREA

One reason I swim is the sense of freedom I feel in the water. This sensation of unbounded-ness, of unrestrained fluidity, is even more pronounced when at the water's edge lies a fenced-in land of captivity. The Yalu River separates the hermit kingdom of North Korea from China, and it was in the Yalu that I swam, just upstream of the crane-sprouting Chinese city of Dandong, on a clear October morning.

As I spat into my goggles a few steps from the water, to my surprise, nine men and one woman walked down the embankment in their swimsuits, put on fins and high-tech hand paddles, and started to slide into the river. A few smiled at this stranger in trunks, and one of them, short and muscular, with a clutter of teeth and circular fire-cupping imprints across his back, signaled for me to get in the water next to him. He later told me his name was Yi Hong Fung.

Most of the swimmers gradually dispersed in the direction of the far shore, about five hundred meters away. But Yi and I swam together, alternating between freestyle and breaststroke, occasionally testing each other's speed. I felt light and fast, and probably could have quickly outdistanced him despite his paddles and fins (much of my youth was spent in competitive swimming), but this was not a race. And I didn't know whether the swimmers were going to pass the river's midpoint, the official boundary, or veer back toward the Chinese shore.

Answer: we stroked all the way to the far bank and landed a bit downstream because of the current. Yi stood in the North Korean mud and warmed up in the sunlight. I needed the sun too. You can imagine the water was cold, yes, but it was bearable because of our exertion, and to my surprise, it seemed clean—no litter, suds, turds, or taste of diesel. We stood next to a four-meter-high fence of ragged netting held up by poles that looked like scavenged tree branches—North Korea's protection against invading swimmers and escaping citizens.

The riverbank was a gradual rise of swamp grass; twenty meters from where we'd landed there was a small white shack—a North Korean guard station. There were no visible gun-toting Democratic People's Republic of Korea soldiers here, as there had been the day before at the upstream trickle of a Yalu branch at Tiger Mountain.

There, Chinese minders and the DPRK personnel threatened gunfire at anyone trying to take a picture of the soldiers. Here, no one. Silence.

Yi and I had been the first of the group to reach the far shore; others smiled at me as they arrived. Their skin glowed with the orange color of the early sun. I punched Yi's shoulder and said "*hun hao*" (very good) to praise his strength. He made a similar gesture to acknowledge mine.

After we plodded through the mud for a while, I motioned to Yi for us to swim back to our starting point, now upriver. "*Bu shi.*" This meant no, and with a sweep of his hand he indicated that the current would be too strong, we'd have to aim for a downstream point. It was all part of his regular circuit, I supposed.

Here we are: Yi and I, planted in the shallows of arguably the least-free country in the world, a fenced pen holding in millions through a combination of despotism, punishing violence, and enforced mind-control ideology.

Yi was free, free to do this whenever he wanted, although I guess he didn't recognize the mockery he made, with every swim, of the hermit tyrant ruling the far shore. But Yi lives in China. The West would say he is not really free, either, that he is a citizen of a country controlled by an illegitimate, information-suppressing party—a self-engendered corrupt network of pseudo-communists.

But on this morning, with Yi's toothy smiles and exuberance, the simple freedom of swimming seemed the only concern of both of us.

As we swam back to the Chinese shore, Yi turned his head now and then to make sure I hadn't been swept too far by the current. We sprinted the last hundred meters, perhaps racing, perhaps just trying to beat the current to our mark on the other side—a stretch of riverside stone steps where clothes were being washed by a group of women.

Yi and I shook hands on the steps. He seemed as energized as I was, with a robustness bordering on joy. "*Xie xie*," I thanked him. He replied the same.

I walked about a kilometer upriver to where I'd left my clothes. I strolled slowly, to give myself more time to think about freedom.

CULTURAL REVOLUTION
OR CULTURAL DECAPITATION?

I 'll change her name to Ms. Wang, so she won't risk retribution from the government. On an overcast November day, Ms. Wang, early forties, guided me through one of the historically important cities of central China. She was poised, professional, competent, but slightly pre-programmed in her commentaries about the landmarks of the ancient city. She was much more fluid of thought and speech when I asked if her family had been affected by the Cultural Revolution. It turned out that yes, they had been, very much so. As we rode in a surprisingly comfortable taxi from one site to another across the city, she was patient with my questions and told me some of her family history.

In the 1960s, Ms. Wang's father, an engineer in the People's Liberation Army, was transferred from his home in central China to Aksu, in Xinjiang province, the far west of China. His assignment there was to help build factories. On a home visit during his early years there, he met his future wife and took her with him back to Aksu.

During the Cultural Revolution, Ms. Wang's father was imprisoned in Xinjiang as an "anti-revolutionary person" because he was well educated. He was locked up in 1969, at the tail end of the worst part of the "revolution," and was released in 1974 when the Gang of Four was ousted. Originally 185 centimeters tall (just over six feet), after his incarceration he was significantly shorter; he could no longer stand up straight, his vertebrae having been broken during repeated beatings on his spine with poles and hammers. Later, as a free man, whenever the weather changed he would be the first to know, in his bones. He told his daughter he was more accurate than the weatherman.

Who beat Ms. Wang's father in prison? The youths of the Red Guard—the violent social movement of young people unleashed by Mao. They would tell the prison chief that they needed to ask technical questions of certain prisoners to make sure the factories could keep working. This was their excuse to interrogate selected prisoners, and to beat them. Torture seems the appropriate term here. Ms. Wang illustrates their questioning by pointing at the headrest of the taxi driver in front of her: "What color is this?" they would ask. "It's gray." "No, it's black. Now look again. What color is it?" "It's gray." "No, it's black." They would punish the victim until the "right" answer came out.

After his release from prison Ms. Wang's family was compensated for her father's five years of incarceration. They received precisely the salary he would have been paid during those missing years, nothing more.

Although Ms. Wang's father remained in poor health after his release, he did return to work. At age fifty-nine, in the late 1990s, he died of a heart attack. His fate was not as bad as that of many of his fellow inmates, though: several committed suicide while in prison. Ms. Wang tells me that her father was brave, perhaps trying to explain to herself why he did not also kill himself. She is unsentimental in her tone as she says this.

I ask if other families she knew also suffered during this time. The father of Ms. Wang's close school friend was forced by the Red Guards' threats to flee to nearby Pakistan; only several years later did he return to his family. Ms. Wang said she was told that other family acquaintances were murdered during this period.

I ask if Ms. Wang's father was angry after his imprisonment. "Yes." And her mother? Less angry, but she was worn down by the poverty of their life in Xinjiang, which Ms. Wang was too young to remember. (Doing the math, if her dates are correct, Ms. Wang was born shortly after her father was imprisoned.) According to her mother, who continued to work during her husband's absence and was paid a very basic salary, they subsisted on cabbage and tofu and little else. Cooking was done in a mud hearth in the corner. No electricity, so oil lamps were used at night. "It was a very hard life, my mother told me."

Ms. Wang says Deng Xiaoping is the real hero for China, because of his "economic opening." She adds that "Chairman Mao is still liked by many people, but Zhou Enlai [premier under Mao] was the better leader. Mao liked pretty girls. He had many wives, like an emperor." Ms. Wang's mother had to read Mao's Little Red Book and recite from it. Ms. Wang even remembers a couple of lines and says teachings like "good is the commune" sound funny to her now.

According to Ms. Wang, rich people in China can have more than one child, contrary to the well-known rules about one child per family. The rich simply pay to beat the regulations. She described how it works: the parents hand over about thirty thousand yuan (US$4,800) to a doctor in a hospital to certify that their firstborn child has a medical disorder that permits them to have a second child. Ms. Wang says corruption like this, in other settings, is commonplace. It is obvious she is not a rabble-rouser or activist—merely telling the truth after a long day.

Ms. Wang herself has only one child, a daughter in the final year of high school. The daughter wants to go to Shanghai or Beijing for university studies and to pursue economics, finance, or architecture. Ms. Wang sometimes must travel within China for work, but after a few days on the road she always wants to get back home to see her child.

I wonder how much Ms. Wang's daughter knows about her family's history during the Cultural Revolution. Within China, the topic is banned from textbooks and censored on the internet. If Ms. Wang's daughter knows the family history, then she also knows it is forbidden to discuss it openly. On the other hand, if she doesn't know the history, perhaps because Ms. Wang wants to protect her daughter from the awfulness of it, then daughter and mother live, in a way, in parallel worlds. In either case, there is a wall of silence that is replicated across the millions of Chinese families who suffered in similar ways during this devastating "revolution."

I later discussed this with a thoughtful Chinese man from Beijing who works for the Ministry of Foreign Affairs. He says that the topic is banned because of the divisions that might occur if the people who suffered were to seek retribution. I counter that the Chinese Communist Party probably bans it because the facts are so damaging to its reputation. He doesn't respond to my assessment, but gravely acknowledges that denial carries a big danger: if the horrors of that period are never acknowledged, then young people will never learn the lesson of the tragedy—which is the first step toward repeating it.

FLAMES ON A HOT DAY

An hour past midday and an outdoor assembly of
Laotians and I move like a herd to escape the
smoke from a bonfire. We are on the grounds
of a Buddhist temple, a *wat*, and the bonfire is a funeral
pyre. Women and men cover their mouths with cloth,
their faces suggesting that more than being worried about
smoke in their lungs, they fear inhaling the emissions,
and maybe the spirit, of the corpse. Ashes rain down on
us, speckling everyone's black hair with flecks of white.

A short while earlier, while saffron-robed monks
chanted and prayed in the subtropical heat, a young Lao
woman standing next to me explained in bashful English
what was happening... and what had happened.

The Lao lady, poised and somber, is a cousin of the
dead man's wife. The deceased was thirty-eight, worked
at the airport, and, judging by the couple of hundred
people present, had many friends and relatives. Two days
earlier, he and his wife were hit by a car while on a

moped. The wife lies in the hospital with head wounds and limb fractures.

Because the death was by accident rather than disease, the family, believing that their home would be haunted by the deceased's spirit, did not bring him home first to pay their final respects. Instead, following Buddhist tradition, the body went straight to the care of monks at the temple.

The young woman next to me says that unlike death by accident, death by disease can be assuaged when a young man or woman of the deceased's family becomes a monk or a nun for a time; this results in the dead person's elevation to a higher status in the next turn of the wheel of life. Death by accident offers no such option—only the prayers of monks already ordained can provide a possible promotion in the next reincarnation.

Following the monks' prayers and chants, the casket, with a small wood-frame tower atop, painted white with flowery gold trim and peaked by a hand-fashioned cupola, is moved from the wat's pavilion into the court-yard, where it is placed on a stone platform. Suddenly, a throng of children runs back and forth in front of the cremation stage—chasing candies thrown into the air by a smiling old man. A reminder that death is binary: either it strikes someone close to you and you grieve, or it happens on the other side of the window pane of caring. Even then, it serves to bring people together.

Flowers are carried to the casket in its new location, where it is opened for viewing so that family members, including the children, can pour onto the body the milk of coconuts, a symbol of purification. The dead man's two children, a boy and a girl, perhaps ten and twelve years old, stand in front of the casket tower with family members and pose for photos. The girl holds a framed portrait of her father and bravely tries to contain her crying.

While the other children chase candies, two wires are strung up between the casket tower and the branches of an old tree in the courtyard. A man fiddles with two colorful cylinders, trying to mount them on the wires. They turn out to be firecracker rockets, each with a thick, yard-long fuse dangling from it.

The deceased's little son, his face streaked with tears, receives two lit candles. A man directs the boy's shaky hands to the fuses. Sparks appear, followed by hissing and whistles as the rockets streak along the guy wires, hit the casket tower, and explode. The kerosene sprinkled earlier on the casket is slow to ignite. Eventually the fire catches on and blazes, the cupola topples over in flames, and the tower and casket are being consumed.

With the casket now nearly gone, the crowd and I watch for any feature of the body within the flames. The Lao lady motions with her elbow to indicate she can see one of the dead man's arms. Sure enough—it's sticking up, bent, like he's playing a drum. It's blackened,

73

but still stout, as if the flames have only glazed the skin (or maybe the arm has swelled). The Lao lady says the burning doesn't seem to be going so well.

Before long we see the head, too, which also seems to resist the inferno, now amplified by some sort of gas burner underneath. The torso and upper legs are also apparent, even more so when the busy pyre attendant sticks a long bamboo pole beneath the corpse to lever it up, push away debris, and allow the fire to do its business. The pole rocks the stiff, charred body, making its outline clear, indeed. I can see by the gazes of those around me, including the children, that I am not the only one mesmerized by the spectacle.

The Lao woman now tells me the dead man's wife, whom she visited in the hospital just before coming to the temple, does not know her husband is dead. The family is worried that she, too, will die if she learns he did not survive. When she regained consciousness after the accident, she immediately asked about her husband; they told her he was recovering in a different room. "As soon as I can walk, I want to see him," she insisted.

But her husband, the father of her children—what is left of him in this turn of the wheel—now burns slowly on a hot Sunday afternoon in Vientiane, under the watchful eyes of his offspring and a crowd of onlookers who are certain of his fate.

I think of the little girl crying, holding a portrait of her father, and I try to imagine what she will remember of this day many years from now. And I think of my own little daughter.

FRESH PAPERS

Tina was losing what little patience she had left. Her boss kept pushing back the date for her to fly across the Persian Gulf to Kish, in Iran, to renew her work visa. First it was to be December 18th. Then the 22nd. She was coming up on six months now, six long months tending bar in Dubai, living in a shared plaster house surrounded by bulldozed roads and newly made curbs. She caught herself barking at customers and occasionally tormenting the impatient men trying to order a drink, ignoring them until they were furious; Tina chided herself for succumbing to all the bartender habits that had disturbed her when she first arrived in the Emirates. Her few friends, other white South African workers like herself, were planning a Christmas party that promised to relieve the bleakness. They were all in their twenties, like her, recruited to serve the tourists flocking to the hotels rising in great numbers along the pristine beaches that rimmed the empty, sandy land.

Her friends began taunting her when December 22nd had passed. "Don't worry, Tina, Saint Nick will come visit you in Iran," they teased. "He even has the full beard, so they'll be sure to let him in."

At last she got the go-ahead, on Christmas Eve. The midday flight across the gulf took less than an hour; below the plane the endless, bland haze on the sea was pierced here and there by oil derricks.

Tina's boss had told her to take a big shawl and head covering. "You should have no problem over there," he'd said. "It's a little permit factory and it works. You and the others go in, stay overnight, get new visas the next day, and leave. Just keep covered up."

Tina was herded through the Kish airport along with the other workers, collected from a dozen countries, who had all funneled into the Emirates for the jobs and the cash. They outnumbered the Dubai locals by nine to one: maids, receptionists, cooks, janitors, waitresses, drivers. Not slaves by any means, but slaving for their families back home and their intertwined futures. Their work visas required them to exit the country every six months, so by the planeload they made the same periodic hop across the gulf to the closest Emirates consulate, in Kish, to apply for fresh working papers. Tina gave her passport to the visa fixer waiting in the arrivals hall, and then she was shuttled to a dormitory room to be shared with an Egyptian, an Indian, and a slender young Pakistani woman named Salima who had sat next to Tina on the plane.

"I can't believe we have to be here over Christmas," Tina said as the girls tossed their small travel bags onto the bunk beds. Two of her roommates looked up in surprise. "Then again," she smiled sheepishly, "I suppose that might not matter much to you."

"Is today Christmas?" asked Muminah, the young woman from Cairo, in lilting English.

"No, it's tomorrow," said Salima. "Tina told me on the airplane."

"Yup, perfect timing." Tina looked around the small room, lit by two fluorescent ceiling lights. The room was like a sealed box with only a single, tiny window. "Hey—I saw the beach from the van. Anybody for a walk?"

Only Salima was willing and the deskman watched her and Tina as the two of them left the building, mumbling to himself as their long over–dresses lifted slightly on the new concrete steps, exposing one ankle each.

There were only a few men on the streets, in leather jackets that seemed too heavy for the warm weather. And there was no one on the beach, a ribbon of platinum blonde cut at the near end by a rock jetty and at the other end by a forest of cranes and smokestacks, just silhouettes in the glare. Tina squatted to pick up a shiny, fist-sized shell embedded with swirls of amber, white, and red. She showed it to Salima, who took it in her hands and turned it over several times in silence.

"Tina," she finally said, "you have found something very beautiful." She handed it back and they continued walking.

"It's so hot, Salima. Don't you get tired of all this...all this stuff we have to slog around in?"

"It is normal. I grew up with it. I like it."

They walked in a meandering path just above the line where the dry sand gave way to wet.

"I want to take off our shoes," Tina said. "That's the only way to walk on a beach." She bent down suddenly, grabbing at Salima's canvas sneakers.

"No! Stop that!" Salima was laughing but planted her feet firmly.

"Okay, but mine are coming off," Tina said, peeling off her black flats. She skipped into the timid waves, wetting her skirts.

"Put them back on or I will leave. I like walking on the beach with you, but...."

Tina sauntered out of the water, put her hand on Salima's shoulder, and hopped on one foot as she pulled the shoes back on.

"Do you have a boyfriend, Salima?"

"At home, in Pakistan, there are no boyfriends."

"And in Dubai?"

Salima said nothing, then smiled and reached for the scarf that had slipped off Tina's head onto her shoulders.

They heard a scream, an angry scream. A man outside a nearby rusty building ran a few paces toward them, his arms in the air, his gray-and-black tunic shaking.

"What's he saying?"

"Your head was uncovered, Tina. Make sure it doesn't slip again!"

Tina knotted the cloth tightly beneath her chin. The man continued shouting.

"Tell me what he's saying."

"I think he is saying bad things. About you. He is very religious. Let's go back."

They turned around quickly and trudged in the sand toward the jetty, then turned up the path to the dormitory. *The barracks*, thought Tina. Muminah and Fadma, the young woman from India, were still in the room, one reading, the other listening to music through her earphones. Dinner was early, downstairs. Back in the room Salima, Muminah, and Fadma prayed, and then the lights went out. Beneath the sheets Tina removed her clothes, down to her underwear.

Tina was the last to awake in the morning. As she pulled the pillow over her face to block the light hovering just above her in the upper bunk, she heard giggles. She rolled to peer over the edge of the mattress and saw her three companions seated on stools around the small table, in the center of which was a tiny cake with a large red candle. The lit candle was too big for the cake and threatened to topple over.

"Happy Christmas, Tina," said Salima, then all three said, "Happy Christmas."

"*Oooh*...thank you!" Tina sat up abruptly and the sheet fell from her shoulders, revealing her bra. The three looked at each other, then again at Tina. Their embarrassment broke into laughter. Tina laughed too.

"Just a minute." Tina jumped down from the bed, holding her wad of clothes, and put them on.

"Girls, girls. Thank you. Merry Christmas." She leaned over to kiss each one on the cheek.

"Tina, sing us the songs," said Fadma.

"Yes, Tina, the Christmas songs," Muminah and Salima chimed in.

"Ah, I can't sing." The eyes around her said *please*.

"Oh, what the hell. Okay, 'Jingle Bells.'" She sang "Jingle Bells" and gradually coaxed the others to sing along with her. Tina picked her keys out of her purse and rattled them like bells to the tune. Their voices all grew to full volume. Tina danced while imitating a sleigh driver. She tried to pull the others up to dance but they resisted, still singing verse after repeated verse. Tina finished off the song with a full-throated crescendo that ended with all four applauding.

"Tina, what about...a song about the Jesus baby," said Salima, glancing at Muminah and Fadma.

"I'm not so good on the religious stuff," said Tina. "I've only been to church a few times. Christmas is for fun and family, and today you are my family."

But the expectant eyes were on her again. She started to sing "Silent Night" but soon stumbled, searching for the words after "all is calm, all is bright."

"Okay, okay, 'White Christmas,'" Tina said. She brought the others into the song, fluttering her fingers in the air like falling snowflakes.

When it was over she said, "Now, sisters, it's time for you to sing. Sing me any song."

The other girls grimaced but Tina saw Salima look sideways, biting her lip.

"Salima! Sing. Sing!" Tina pounded the table. The two other girls rapped their fingers lightly.

"Yes, Salima. Sing for us." Fadma started pounding the table too.

There was a long pause. Salima looked up at the ceiling. The first tone was high-pitched and piercing, but her voice soon dipped and careened between halftones, then rose and fell in cycles, her lips stretched wide as if smiling. Her voice was pure and reverberated between the stark walls, obliterating the blankness of the room.

Tina had tears in her eyes when Salima finished.

"What is it about?" she asked.

"It's from home. A boy is in love with a girl. He wants to touch her long, black hair. He thinks it is beautiful. And he thinks *she* is beautiful."

The four young women spent the day walking together in the dusty lanes near the dormitory, occasionally venturing into shops, speaking quietly among themselves. They caught the inspecting stares of men, the young ones wearing smart western jackets, the older ones in full-length tunics.

The women were standing among fabrics hanging from a store awning when Salima touched Tina's back and whispered, "That's him." Tina turned around.

"That's who?"

"The man who was yelling at you. On the beach." Salima slowly nudged aside a woolen drape so the two of them could see across the lane. He was picking up something wrapped in paper at a food stall and turned his head toward them as he wedged it into his mouth. Salima quickly let the drape fall to cover them.

"You're right."

"Let's stay here for a while until he goes away," said Salima.

"Stay here in our little prison, sure. No. I want to walk."

"Tina." Salima grabbed her hand and pulled hard.

"Okay. For you, Salima." The four women remained hiding behind the curtains of cloth for sale. Salima pinched Tina twice on the elbow when Tina's voice rose above a whisper. At last Salima said, "Let's look again, then we'll go." When they stepped out into the open lane the sun was low and blinding; they walked directly toward it, four abreast, close together.

"It's such a pretty day, such a lovely Christmas Day. Let's walk down to the beach." Tina took Fadma's and Muminah's hands and started to skip, tugging without success. Only Salima agreed to go with her. "All right, Tina, just for a little bit. But keep your shoes on." They parted from the others in front of the dormitory.

On the beach Tina noticed for the first time the milk cartons, plastic bags, and spent motor oil containers strewn in patches across the sand.

"Tell me more about the boy in Dubai. I met a guy there from Bulgaria. His eyes are so dark and I love his skin. He's a wild dancer. Tell me, Salima."

"Mmm. Tina. It's too private."

The two women did not walk as far up the beach as they had the day before. They talked about their families, their brothers and sisters, and slowly made their way back.

On the steps of the dormitory, Tina sat down. It was dusk.

"I can't go back to that little room yet."

"But Tina, there is nothing to do out here. And they take us to the airport in an hour or two anyway. You can relax when we're back in Dubai tonight."

"Just a little while. I'll come up soon."

Tina sat wondering if there would be any Christmas party stragglers left by the time she got back to Dubai. Surely by now they were all ripped on vodka and tequila. She stood up and walked in a slow circuit around the squat dormitory building, stepping over animal droppings in the narrow alleyway of packed dirt. *How had she ended up in a place like this?* she wondered. How had she, living in a hilly green heaven on earth at the far end of Africa, where she had good friends, gotten so off track that she ended up not only alone in a desert city on the other side of the world, but in this putrid alley tripping over dung on Christmas Day? It disgusted her. She became nauseated and hurried down the long alley toward the front door. But as she turned the next-to-last corner, a sudden force crushed her shoulder into the wall of the dormitory building, ripping the neck seam of her dress and dragging the scarf off her head. Before she could shout, the rough wool was on her mouth, digging into her lips and skin. One of his arms was behind her neck; the elbow of the other arm was jammed into her face. He pressed her against the wall and wrenched her head to bring her whole body down, releasing her mouth

86

for an instant. She screamed and then felt the blow to her ear. He was on top of her, pressing all the breath out of her. She could see only the edge of the wall against the violet sky. Tina thought she was drowning, drowning in sand. His beard was like sand, suffocating her.

She pounded on him and her pounding did nothing. Breathe, breathe. She tried to kick but her legs would not move under his weight—or was it because she had no air? She frantically stabbed her right hand into the pocket that held the shell from the beach. She felt one of his hands clawing at her pubis, ripping the underwear. The wall-edged patch of sky was fading now as her vision scattered into arcs of short-lived light. Time seemed to be taking forever. In half-consciousness she felt her hand on the shell. She clenched it and swung it to his face, so hard that it tore open his cheek, cracked, and continued its trajectory into her own forehead. The broken edge of the shell remained in his flesh. He grabbed the hand that had hit him, leaving her mouth free, but there was no air with which to scream.

Yet there was a scream. And more screams. The man jerked his head up and leapt to his feet. Salima and Fadma and Muminah were at the far end of the lane with the dormitory deskman. Soon there were others. The man was holding his hand to his face; he shouted and pointed his finger at Tina, panting on the ground. A policeman ran up to them both; behind him was the visa fixer.

"He says you offered yourself to him," said the visa man. Tina could not speak; she was still gasping. The policeman glared at her. He seemed to know the man in the gray-and-black robe, whom Tina now at last could see. Salima ran to her, knelt, and held her by the shoulders.

"If she offered herself, why is there blood coming from his face!" yelled Salima, pointing at the man's head. The visa fixer translated and pointed also. The policeman grabbed the man's wrist and pulled his hand away from his cheekbone, uncovering the deep gash that now was bleeding freely. The policeman shouted at him, then the two argued fiercely, the policeman holding the other man's forearm as he tried to twist free.

The visa fixer pulled Salima and Tina up from the ground.

"We have to go. Come. Now!"

From the van as they drove away, the four girls could see the policeman and the man in the gray-and-black tunic still shouting at each other as the onlookers were slipping off to both ends of the darkening street. Tina shivered and leaned against Salima, who held her hand and whispered, "We heard you through the window."

On the plane, when they were gliding high over the gulf, Salima placed another tissue against the trickle of blood on Tina's forehead where it had been cut by the shell. "I think you will have a scar here. I am sorry, Tina. Very sorry."

88

Tina felt her row of three joined seats shaking slightly and leaned forward to look at Fadma in the seat next to Salima. Fadma's chin was on her chest, and she was crying, crying so much that tears ran in rivulets down to the tip of her nose, where they formed quickly falling drops.

Salima put her mouth to Tina's ear and whispered. "Fadma...Fadma, last year...."

Tina released her seat belt and reached across Salima to grasp Fadma's cold and shaking hands. Tina's lips trembled and her head tumbled, sobbing, into Salima's lap.

YOUR ETERNITY

"**S**o you think you've got immortality wired," said Sasha, always the skeptic except when she was in bed. "And you don't even believe in souls."

"Not *that* kind," said Justin. "I've got more practical ideas, more ambitious. I just wish I'd figured it out sooner, how to capture me for eternity before now. I mean, my soul will be missing its first twenty-four years."

This wasn't the first time Justin had sounded grandiose, thought Sasha, and she let it slide. After four tempestuous months together, she grudgingly admitted to herself that one of the attractions of this relationship was Justin's techno-mysticism; his detailed plan slightly aroused her.

"The gear's all there—the temple-mounted minicams, the micro audio samplers, the giga storage that'll fit on my thumbnail," said Justin. "And of course you can edit the hell out of it over beers, and we'll even shoot that, too, the editing."

"We? Who is *we*?"

"I can't run the cameras *only* by myself. I mean, like, my arm's only so long. So I gotta have a technician, a handy-grip, otherwise eternity won't see me, my face, my expressions, my mannerisms...my soul. Got it, princess?"

She got it, but her mind was spinning forward. Sasha didn't want to share him. She had developed a mild jealousy on their second night together, when she'd named him Just-in-Time Justin because of the synchrony of their lovemaking. "So, maybe you want me to be your handy-grip."

"Whoa. What about when we're locked in mouth-to-mouth and going for it? There's gotta be a third party, otherwise we lose that *vignette privée*—that tender piece of my propagated soul." Justin grinned.

"You mean you want someone else to tape us in the sack?" The thought intrigued her.

"Yep, gotta get it all, minute by minute. That's the point. For eternity's sake. But you and me in bed is such a small part of it. There's my thoughts too. I'll talk about them into the mike as I navigate," said Justin.

Sasha raised her brown caterpillar eyebrows. "Navigate *what*?"

"Navigate life—*my* life. And then outload it all. It's gotta be formatted in every digital standard out there. We might even backtrack to analog, in case extraterrestrials are still fudging with that. It's gotta be fully dispersible, and the archival's gotta be durable as gold.

Do you know if there's anything other than analog and digital? I've gotta cover all the bases. It's immortality we're talking about. You don't want to mess it up."

"But you can't capture all of it," said Sasha.

"Come on. The technology's here! I'll get every second. I'm even going to record my dreams when I wake up in the morning."

"And who's going to bother to look at the minutiae of your life? I mean, it could be worse than reading an encyclopedia...or a dictionary...or the yellow pages...or Proust." Justin liked Sasha's piercing comments, but he generally tried to ignore them.

"I've gotta find someone to help with the editing too," he continued. "Then I'll send it all out—I mean various edited versions of it—on commercial multi-spectrum transmitters to the far reaches of the universe, maybe beyond. And once those deep space radio signals go out, it's forever, baby; it just keeps going. Light years and light years of immortality. Do you know you can rent satellite channel time to far space for a pittance now?"

"For you it's a pittance, thanks to your parents."

"But that's the natural generational result, for the far-minded," said Justin. "Take John Adams—he dedicated himself to politics and war so his sons could learn navigation and commerce so their sons could dibble-dabble in poetry and music. He left out the next phase—the sons who would transmit their souls to the universe. Daughters too. And about your yellow pages complaint: hell, way out there they'll be starved for this kind of stuff. First contact—they'll lap it up, like those home confinement shows on TV down here. But, baby, this is between you and me. If word gets out, there'll be a race, and then all the clutter would...."

"Drown out your immortality?" Sasha's expression seemed slightly wicked.

"It's not like that exactly. There's space for everybody. But *first* carries a premium. Like Plato—now there's a guy who knew how to transmit over time and space. Get the message recorded and get it out. And besides, some souls are more immortal than others. It's like those plant species imported to foreign continents where they have no natural competitors and take over. That's why I've gotta send it out in as many formats as possible—you never know the niche in which your soul will best propagate. I want pollen, spores, seeds of me spread everywhere."

"Well, Plato, if it doesn't have any big ideas attached, won't the at-home series fizzle out after a while, like all one-shot wonders do?" She arched her eyebrows. Checkmate.

"I'm ahead of you, my smooch." Justin winked. "Here's the fix: the digital composites of my soul will have subprograms attached, like viruses. Call them my gifted replicons. You've seen those programs that generate poems or plots with a few keystrokes? The repl-icons will generate new permutations based upon my soul data set. As for big new ideas—that's just a matter of semi-random associations subjected to selective pressures. The viruses will spew their stuff out and some will stick, with my name and personality attached. Haven't you heard about all the garbage even the greatest thinkers have pumped out? Dustbin ideas. Only the precious leftovers made them great minds in retrospect. So yeah, a lot of the ether spume fails, but the good little leftover soul-frags survive and propagate. Call it soulful universal evolution." Justin was pleased with his phraseology, and it showed.

"Why not just concentrate on Earth, where at least you know you have listeners? Like in places without media saturation?"

"Oh gawd, Sasha. I *could* focus on all those humans in no-man's-land with nothing to watch except a satellite feed, and send my soul data train out to them, which of course I'd have translated into the native tongue—that's a super-trivial software deal now: Greek in, Pashto out, any combination. Yeah, I could do all that. The problem, my little sushi Sasha, is that the *Earth* is *not* the *future*. The future is out there! In Sagittarius or Scorpio or Orion or...you pick your favorite patch of sky. My soul is for them! I live for *them*, out there!"

"I suppose having children doesn't get you your immortality? Earth children?" Sasha was on firm, unbiased ground here, since she'd said innumerable times that she had no interest in having any kids herself.

"Children, nah. Not that kind of seed. I'm not a control freak. Children fly away and they should. Even the genetics argument is a waste—after two generations, the DNA mixing dilutes me to nothing. I know where you're headed, Sasha." Justin rocked on the rear legs of his chair, catching himself as he almost tumbled backwards. "Of *course* I've thought about clones. And I'm sure you've seen those stories about identical twins separated at birth who are shocked when they reunite at age fifty, and they have the same beer bellies and are both firemen. The press selects for those examples; the fact is, even with the same DNA, my clones would grow up different from me. For all I know, my clones would become con artists or chemical engineers, and where would that leave my soul? Clones are too dicey. I'd rather bet on several eager viruses that have my data strapped on like jetpacks, ready to permutate my posterity."

Sasha wouldn't acknowledge to herself that she was, in fact, attracted to his pomposity. But immortality... *that* she could admit was alluring, though she had her doubts about intelligent beings way out there.

"And what happens to the other...factors...in what gets transmitted?" she asked.

"You mean the people I meet? You mean you? Yeah, you mean you." Justin started to roll his eyes.

"For example," said Sasha.

"Look, you're part of me. You're in there—in my soul for the ether. And gawd, we spend a lot of time together."

"And all that editing you talked about?" Sasha tried to keep her voice detached and clinical, but it was beginning to buckle.

"There'll be zillions of bytes of you in there. The universe will know me and so it will know you. You're in there. You *will* be in there."

"And the replicons? Will they take me along...."

"For the ride? Wow! I hadn't thought about that. Huh. Hmm."

There was a long silence between them. Justin looked up toward the ceiling. Sasha examined his face.

"I guess it's like a will," he said. "You can change it up to the end."

"You mean you're going to start transmitting only at the end, when you're dying?"

"Sasha, you're ahead of me here, you wizard. I'm not a control freak, you know. But I guess, hmm...I guess I'd want revision rights up to the end."

"And so we...you...you lose all that lead time the longer you live. Time for the clutter to spread across the universe, time for someone else to be first. You're young. That's a lot of lead time to give up," said Sasha.

"Um, yeah, the lead time. Tick tock. I'd better gear up quick and start beaming. You never know when a bus will flatten me or some jerk will beat me to the punch. So I...I suppose your soul is along for the ride too." He kissed her, Sasha kissed him back, and the two grappled their way to the couch where they joined themselves amid tender thoughts a thousand years in the future, when they would long be dead, maybe.

★ ★ ★

In the morning Justin groaned and pulled a pillow over his face to block out the light. He had a hard-on and groped his hand across the bed. The other side was empty.

"Sasha. Sasha! Are you in the toilet?"

There was no answer. He lugged himself out of bed and walked to the living room, his organ pointing the way. He barely saw her silhouette against the glaring sunshine streaming through the unwashed windows. "What are you doing?" Justin wanted to sound imperious, but it came out as a whimpering complaint. He rubbed the night's mucous from his eyes and blinked.

Sasha was seated at the foldout table, wearing a Japanese robe. She was writing in a leather-bound book.

"Sasha?"

"I'm busy. Why don't you make us some tea? Pear and vanilla would be fine." Her pen kept moving and she didn't look up.

"What are you doing?" Justin tumbled onto the couch and buried his face between the cushions.

"Waiting for tea."

He raised his head and looked over the arm of the couch. Sasha's long brown hair was draped across her cheek and swayed with the motion of her hand. "All right, all right." Justin cracked his knee against the coffee table on his way to the kitchen but refused to yelp. As he heated the water his aggravation rose in proportion to the retreat of his organ.

"Here's the tea, for thee, my queen. Now what *is* that?" The cup clicked against the table top and spilled a little next to the book. Sasha snapped it shut and pulled it away from the puddle.

"It's my journal. Sort of a diary, sort of not." Sasha smiled. Justin thought she looked like a Cheshire cat as he hovered over her. He pulled up a chair and sat down.

"And, and, what's in there?"

"This and that. And whatsits and whosits."

"I've never seen it before," said Justin.

"No need to wave it in your face."

"So...do you write in it a lot?"

"Every day."

"Rain or shine?"

"Rain or shine."

"How long?"

"Since I was twelve."

"All the details?"

"All the important ones."

"Since you were twelve?"

"Since I was twelve."

"You've been keeping a journal since you were a little girl and you never told me?" Justin felt completely naked; and he was, except for the pen, which had rolled strategically onto his lap when his agitated legs bumped the table. "And what do you do with it, or with them? You must have a bookcase full."

"I read them. Add a few details now and then." Sasha tugged the book toward her as Justin eyed it. "And edit."

"Everything that happens to you is in there?"

"Yup. Thoughts too."

Justin put the pen back on the table and slowly rubbed his face. "Am I in there?"

"Maybe. A little bit."

Justin scratched his thighs and reached for the shirt he had shed on the floor the night before. He put it on. "Can I read it?"

"No." Sasha planted her elbow on the book.

"So who's read them? Who's *going* to read them?"

"No one. No one but me."

She resumed her writing and purred. At least it sounded like a purr to Justin. He kissed her on the neck. "Please, Sasha. I promise—yours can ride along."

"Okay, maybe, sometime. Just a peek."

A SHOT ON THE ICE

a story for nieces and nephews

A long time ago the Inuit got guns. It made hunting much easier. No more bow and arrow needed, and you didn't have to sneak up as carefully or as closely if you wanted to get a sea lion or even, maybe, a polar bear. The big white bear that could scrape your head off your neck with one wave of its paw.

It was in those days that Sanu the Inuit got his first gun and let his bow and his arrows and his harpoon lie forgotten in the fireplace ashes and grimy ice on the floor of his igloo. *At last I will get a bear,* thought Sanu. The big white bear that could run up behind you so fast and so quietly that you wouldn't have time to turn around. All you would see would be the snowy ground suddenly hitting you in the face. And then you'd be dinner.

Sanu set out on a gray day with his black-barreled gun to get a white bear. That fur and fat, meat and bones would take care of him through the winter. And those big paws—he would show them to everyone he met as he sledded with his dogs, and even strangers would stare and look at him with envy.

This hunt was a one-man job, no dogs, no sled, no noise, no smells. He had to sneak up with the wind just right. It was a long hike. Hours and hours across the ice, hopping over big blocks of it, sinking into snow it had trapped, until he reached the living edge of it, where the ice always fought with its cousin the sea. Here Sanu felt his breathing quicken as he concentrated on the horizon of ice, searching for its edges and the quiet water that would freeze you in the time it took to think of your grandmother's first name. He was searching for the white bear too. The bear that liked this jagged zone and had no fear of the dark water with no bottom. He played in it, dove down deep, and snapped up his food there.

When a bear like that walked on the ice, he flopped his paws and skidded a little as his big long body—as long as two people end to end—swayed left and right in a goofy way that would make you laugh if it weren't so dangerous for him to hear you laughing. But in the water he was as fluid and graceful as the sea lions he chased.

Sanu leaned against an ice boulder and just stayed there, motionless except for his eyes, which roamed slowly left, then right, then left. Nothing. He crouched and made his way to another white boulder closer to the water, where loose beds of ice rubbed each other and made strange sounds. *Grrungrrung. Grrungrrung. Broim. Grrung.*

There! The Bear! He was walking in a big circle on a raft of jumbled ice, looking into the water as he lumbered. *He's looking for food, just like me,* thought Sanu. *He's big. And loooong.* Sanu planted his elbows gently in a mound of snow and pressed his belly against it as he brought the gun near his eye and looked down the long line of greasy steel. The bear lay down and rolled on his side. Was he scratching his back?

Sanu was irritated that a few lumps of hard blue-white snow hid the bear's big back and chest; it wasn't a good shot. He waited. The bear's four legs were up in the air, tilting and shaking as if he were dancing upside down.

Suddenly the giant animal was up on his feet, and before Sanu could adjust his aim the bear splashed into the water and disappeared. *Such a chance, and it's lost,* thought Sanu. The hunter walked a few steps to a flat patch of ice and sat down cross-legged, his head hanging in disappointment. With one of his furry mittens he idly flicked snow off the glassy hardness that separated him from the waters below. *The ice in this spot is clear as glass,* he thought, *about as thick as a foot is long.* Sanu scraped off more of the snow and soon had a little window looking down into the blackness. He lifted his head and gazed at the place where the bear had been, then far to the left, and far to the right. There was nothing. But when

105

he hung his head again he found himself staring right at the bear! The big white face was looking up through the glassy ice at Sanu, smiling, pressing his cheek and nose against Sanu's window. *What luck to be so close!*

Sanu jumped up and put the gun muzzle right on the ice. He held the barrel verticle, like a tent pole, and leaned over to press his shoulder against the wooden stock. Just then a little sunlight broke through the clouds, making the bear's face so clear that Sanu could see his eyelashes. *Was that a wink?*

Boom!

Sanu felt only an instant of pain in his shins before he fell unconscious on the ice. When he woke up he didn't know how long he'd been knocked out, but there was still some light in the sky. His legs were bloody. The gun, what was left of it, was next to his head. The barrel was gone, except for a few twisted metal strands. With the end of the gun pressed against the thick ice, the blast had had nowhere to go, and the gun had exploded, sending its metal into Sanu's legs.

And my face is bloody, thought Sanu, tasting it on his lips. *The ice chips blew back in my face.* But why was his left arm wet and freezing?

The blast had made a long crack in the ice, and Sanu was lying on the edge of a plate of it, as wide as two bearskin rugs, that had broken off and now was drifting into the dark waters, his arm hanging over the side.

Sanu closed his eyes and winced at the pain in his legs. He wiggled his toes. Still on his back, he lifted the right leg, then the left. They worked.

Sanu was shivering. *So why does my face feel like there is a hot breath on it?* He opened his eyes and saw a cloud of vapor coming out of the bear's mouth, just above him. Sanu gasped and held his breath. Some bear slobber dribbled on his forehead.

Sanu lay motionless in his fear. But this white bear didn't seem hungry. Or maybe he didn't like Sanu's smell. Sure, he wanted to play a little, and put a paw on Sanu's chest and tried to roll him over. The paw was so big that it covered Sanu's front all the way down to his belly button. It tickled a little, so Sanu swallowed hard not to make a sound. Sanu wished the big white bear would eat him and get it over with.

But this bear wanted a swim instead, so he flopped and skidded a little to the far side of the ice raft, put his four giant furry paws just on the edge, and leaped into the water. Probably he was smiling.

The force of such a strong and enormous creature jumping... well, Sanu felt it in the sudden tilt of the ice raft, and he thought the whole chunk would tip over and leave him to freeze in the sea. But instead the bear's thrust sent Sanu's little plate of ice drifting slowly back to the shore, where the hunter uncrumpled himself, stood, and struggled homeward.

IMAGICON FARM

Imagination is more important than knowledge.
—ALBERT EINSTEIN

"Okay, double the nutrient beta concentration, switch to zilex psychotropic cocktail, then give a three-phase radiation pulse—no more than thirty seconds." Heath barked the commands impatiently. He was way, way behind schedule on this batch of floating heads. "And get the fruit fly guy in here again—the drosophila whiz. Tell him to meet me in my office, pronto."

Heath was closing the blinds when Tadao came in. "It's too damn bright," said Heath. "Doesn't the janitor know all the far UV and cosmic crap comes right through this glass?"

Tadao said nothing as he stood twirling a lock of long blond hair around his index finger.

"Look, this batch of heads hasn't mutated fast enough," Heath said. "They were doing fine at the embryo stage, all the way up to puberty at eight days, but the thought streams we registered were disappointing. *Banal*, the creative guys said. So we're trying to pick up the pace before their neuroglia and the brain architecture lock up in adulthood. You're supposed to be an expert in making genes do tricks. Got any ideas?"

"Well...at this stage I don't think another radiation pulse will do much good," Tadao said, speeding up his hair twirling. "I'm not a brain guy, but at this late stage, I...I suppose a physical disruption might...force an adventitious reorganization of cortical circuitry, if done under the right perceptual umbrella. But I'm not a brain guy."

"You mean we should give the cabbages—the floating heads—a whack?" Heath was known around the farm as Mr. No Nonsense.

"Well, I would be gentle about it. Who knows what they feel."

"Look, Tadao. Won't a whack just wipe out a few cortical fields, or more, I mean gork them, and set us back two weeks until we can raise another cohort of sprouts? You know how many contracts we have now. And the ova microinjection lab is backed up."

Tadao looked a bit squeamish, thinking about the whacks, and the pressure he was under from a hot-tempered big boss.

"Well...Doctor Heat...."

"It's Heath."

"Yes, Doctor Heath. This may be a bad idea. But something I read...in a research journal from way back— there was a kind of paralysis or palsy or some such. Yes, they called it cerebral palsy. It was brain injury at birth. Many of them developed motor or mental problems, or both. But a small percentage, *don't* ask me why, turned out to be savants. Limited savants, but quite...special. And isn't that what we're selecting for, just a few imaginative oddballs out of a batch of hundreds or thousands?"

"Yeah, but we use mutation and selective pressures to *evolve* imagination on this farm. Not brute force." Heath rubbed his palms across the armrests of his chair.

"Yes, sir," Tadao said, timidly. "But couldn't we say, um, that mutation is just another form of disruption? There's chemical disruption, too, like the broths the cabbages—the heads—float in. I suppose physical disruption...I mean, we've already evolved their itsy bodies down to little bitsy stems. Of course, with only a couple hundred of them in the broth, you'd have to disrupt them each in a different way, to hope that at least a few would yield some knockout marvelous imagination streams. But good gawd, once the glia lock up! The whole crop will just end up in the fertilizer tank." Tadao's nervous squirming now gave the appearance of a little dance, with his hands trying unsuccessfully to find a perch on his hips.

"You have a point," Heath said, turning more contemplative and drawing his finger across his mustache, which was emerald green, a trait his mother had paid extra for, since it was not included in the standard gene palette. "But the disruptions won't be genetically imprinted, so we won't be able to carry over the most useful ones for later reproductive cycles, or even keep the ball rolling with clones."

"Of course that's right, Doctor Heath, sir. Just like back then. Those palsy people produced perfectly normal, I mean ordinary, progeny. But I suppose...I suppose you could keep track of the little blows, the whacks—exactly where they were placed, with the force vectors precisely measured—to know which disruptions gave the fruitful results. That, of course, would have to be supplemented by a standard scanning series to exactly localize the injury...uh, disruption...for later implementation on another set of heads. I hate to say it...." Tadao was suppressing a smile with a smirk, thinking of the implications.

"Go ahead," Heath said.

"Myself being trained in rapid-cycle genetics...yes, some say an expert....I hate to say it, but if it worked, you might not need genetics at all, only a few...whacks. Reproducible whacks, of course. But you really need a brain guy. I'm not a brain guy."

Heath gruffly thanked Tadao, who was relieved and slightly titillated by his own original thinking. Heath watched him skipping down the corridor with a finger twisting his hair, and wondered for the umpteenth time how homosexual genes had survived evolution in spite of being antithetical to reproduction. *Another scientific puzzle*, he thought, but he was grateful for the creative results and had hired as many of Tadao's type as he could, even though they commanded higher wages and plenty of perks.

The brain guy was a woman: O'Leary, in a white coat, who sat down in the chair across from Heath's desk. He'd heard she was carrying on with a young image-capture technician in the visual creations section—a mere technician, and an archivist, even worse. She could do a lot better, Heath thought, especially with that accentuated gluteal curvature her parents had picked out for her.

Heath approached the subject gently, asking how to quickly goose a little more imagination from this late-stage crop.

O'Leary was crisp: "What's the product?"

Heath hesitated. "It's a soft porn, multiplatform, high-plot-content, string-'em-along series. We promised something original, spicy, kinky-but-not-too-kinky."

"You can dial up the hormones. I guess it's all males," she said clinically.

"Let me see," Heath said. He pulled the ova injection chart to his face. "No, thirty-three percent female."

"And they're all in the same broth? All in Syltro A? You're kidding!" O'Leary was visibly offended.

Heath fidgeted. "Yeah, they are, but of course they were segregated up to puberty."

"You soak them in the same hormonal bath and now you want sex streams? And you call this a research outfit? You've got to separate them again and turn up the testosterone in one bath and the . . . . Do you need me to get into hormonal differences, like *male* and *female*?"

"Look, O'Leary, this is a new type of contract for us, outside our bread and butter." Heath was now sure he didn't want to know what she would think about Tadao's little whacks. He pursued a different tack: "Okay, we put them back in male-versus-female hormonal broths. What other options do we have, even as a last resort?"

"Well, there's always the perceptual inputs; maybe the heads haven't gotten adequate stimuli. I've already complained to the stimulus squad that they're not poking at the brains' touch nuclei enough. Some probing like that could be relevant for generating erotic streams, don't you think?" The corners of O'Leary's lips curled upward ever so slightly.

"But the perceptual umbrella guys are so hard to get moving," Heath said. "For them to come up with a new raw stimulus stream would take weeks, at least. We should get rid of the whole lot of fools and just feed in random satellite channel samplings. I know for a fact there's not a single McChen cop film or Rhidonna number in the perceptual guys' whole data hose."

"I can't stand either one," O'Leary interjected before Heath rolled on.

"Any other ways we can shake the pot, stir things up?" he asked, trying to hold his gaze away from O'Leary's curves. "We need some flashes of pizzazz out of these guys. And girls."

"Male versus female...you could...I don't know why we haven't tried this before, at least I don't think so, unless it was by mistake." O'Leary leaned forward in her chair, her face pinched with intrigue; purple and orange braids draped over her radiation monitor badge. "Suppose we put some of the males in the female broth and, you know, vice versa, and then with a subset, switch them back and forth. How long for each exposure, that's the question. You really need an endocrine guy for that. But wait: how much time before the glia lock up?" Now she was on the edge of her seat.

"Uh, six days, maybe seven," Heath said ruefully, with a long exhalation.

"What? Six days? Whoa. You're asking for a miracle. I'd say the only hope is the hormonal switching. Unless you can diggle some more time out of the client."

"It's a defense contract, for the troops who are way up there in orbit, and lonely." Heath circled his hand above his head. "And you know what the financial penalties are with them."

O'Leary rose from her chair. "You've got a hard nut to crack. Excuse me, but I'm late for a consult on a molecular brain scan series—a head that was pinned against the broth efflux grate. There was a lot of damage, but the guys in stream capture are going hog wild with the creative mess it's spewing out. This single imagicon could make, I mean *make*, five contracts at once. But it's gotta be quick. Once those glia lock up, I mean, adult phase... well, I don't need to tell *you*. Good luck!"

It was now apparent to Heath that O'Leary would likely be the one assigned to assess the scans of Tadao's little whacks, if he went ahead with that plan. It concerned him because she might not approve of it, but after a moment's thought, Heath decided that O'Leary was, in the end, a team player.

"What's up?" he said to Clarisse, his secretary, who had just come in and was frowning.

"Dr. Zelko has called three times from Field Seven. They still haven't had a thought stream that shows promise. The capture thugs are complaining."

"Tell him to turn up the touch nuclei probes and corresponding sensors. I'll be down in a few minutes."

Heath sighed as he got out of his chair and pulled his white frock around to cover the erection O'Leary had given him.

Down at Field Seven, Heath gave Zelko the orders for his last-ditch plan: "Segregate the heads into multiple pools, infuse with switched male-female hormonal factors over five days. On days two, three, and four, position subset groups for randomly varied physical disruptions, recording all vector topologies of the blows, and press three heads from each subset against the efflux grate for periods of one, three, and seven hours, marking the affected cortical fields for subsequent scanning."

Zelko liked intricate protocols, and all these commands made him grin, but for this recipe he said he'd need more technicians as well as a mechanical guy to position and operate the titanium hammers that would provide the whacks.

"Get 'em now, *hombre*," Heath said, and Zelko grabbed his phone.

Norquist, the mechanical guy, was a little uneasy with his task the next day, and as he oriented the heads for their little whacks, he said to the cameras mounted on the ceiling, "Do you think they know we're here?" And he initially objected to being the one to hold the chosen few against the efflux grate, because of the accumulating radiation exposure to his hands as he manipulated the positioning rods while the scanners recorded coordinates. But in the end Norquist was promoted, because Heath got what he wanted, and more. They even captured several S&M and gender confusion streams that didn't suit the contract but just might tempt the same client later, or lead to entirely new avenues of diversification.

In his exultation, Heath declared to Clarisse, "I am always astounded by the powers of the human mind."

"You call those cabbage heads human?" Clarisse pressed her chest against Heath's shoulder as she leaned over to see the video screen he was watching. "And besides," she added, pointing at the screen, "I could have thought of that."

★ ★ ★

A few months later, Norquist the mechanical guy received a rambling message from a laser specialist friend based on one of the far-orbital military stations. The laser friend had just downloaded a flick. "It was scary, man...the face was yours, man...your face on a woman with a body to die for. But what they did to her....Hey, dude, you okay down there?"

PUT YOUR DEATH IN THE NEWS

"How will you know when you're too far gone?"
"That's the problem, Kyle." Duke leaned back and scratched a flaking age spot on his broad cranium. "I can see the shaking in my hand. That's easy, no hiding it. But you can't use your own brain to make sure your brain's working right. It'll always tell you everything's just fine even when you look around and don't know what the hell you're doing on that street corner. That's why I'm talking to you, why I wanted to be friends with you. Yeah, you're a good guy but you're also young. Got a sharp mind as far as I can tell. Hell, Kyle, I don't even care that you're into men."

Kyle twisted in his chair. He looked off toward the row of beer taps, like teeth along the bar, and wished the pub's soft reggae were a little louder.

"Ease up, Kyle. You can't fool an old man like me. Unless he's already gone loopy." Duke made a curlicue in the air with his wayward hand and let it land on the brown formica table with a bounce. The frame of his body beneath the plaid flannel shirt was wide but stooped.

"So you like me because I'm young," Kyle said. "You sound like some prowling old gay boy."

"Ah, there's the spark. Glad we're over that." Duke grinned and raised his palm to clap it against Kyle's, but Kyle didn't reciprocate. "I was fine sticking with women until Henrietta died," Duke said, "and she and I held on so long that now it's too late for anything else. Maybe...hah! Maybe you thought I was one of those good-looking prowlers. Well, that is one lightning bolt of a compliment. That's an expression of Henrietta's. The lightning bolt part."

"No, I didn't think you were a prowler," Kyle said. "But then, you always buy the beers."

"What else am I going to spend my dough on? Gigolos like you?" Duke sighed and wiped the beer that drooled out of the sagging left corner of his mouth, hoping Kyle wouldn't see it. "Now don't go all pale-faced on me, Kyle. It was a joke."

"I don't think you have any worries yet. About your brain," Kyle said.

"Well, that's very kind coming from a handsome and intelligent man I have just now accidentally insulted. And I stress the *accidentally*." Duke stared into Kyle's face, trying to get the younger man to meet his gaze. "Come on! You're the blossom of youth and I'm counting on you. We keep meeting now and then, like over the past few months, and guzzle a few, and you tell me how I'm doing."

"And when I spot that you've gone loopy I send you to the guillotine?" Kyle chopped one of his hands like a blade onto the table, mocking the old man.

Duke smiled. "Ah, there's the spark." He paused. "At least I know I'm repeating myself, for now. Yeah, something like that."

"Well, guillotines have been banned for a long time, since even before you were born. And I'm not good with guns, if you want to do it that way."

"So I can't count on you?"

"You could give me a pill to slip into your drink when the time came."

"Ah, Kyle, now you're seeing things my way." Duke clinked his mug against Kyle's and took a long drink.

"But," Kyle said, "I think I'll be waiting a long, long time, especially if I get attached to the idea of you being around."

"You got it, Kyle! That's why it's better you don't like me too much. Remember the insult. Even though it was accidental. The gigolo part."

"So do you know how much I charge for a lay?" Kyle smiled at the flush that spread quickly up Duke's neck. "Nothing less than a thousand unless he's got a monster lamppost." Kyle swished his hand toward the ceiling. Duke thought Kyle's smile had a hint of malice in it.

"Got to think big, I suppose."

"Ah, Duke, there's the spark!" Kyle laughed and lifted his beer. Duke followed. "Just kidding," said Kyle. "Let's get back to you. Think big. Think big about how you'll do it."

"Do what? Oh yeah. That."

"Forget the cyanide in your soup." Kyle clasped his hands together and put his elbows on the table. "Go for drama. Get a mission. You said you're beyond women now, so go for something bigger."

"I'm not into guys."

"But you can still be *flamboyant!*" Kyle flung his arms into the air.

"I'm not a flashy guy, like you fairies."

"But you've only got one death." Kyle nodded to the waitress for another round. "Do you want to dribble out of this world like a puddle of wasted sperm?"

"Wasted sperm? Not me. I've got two kids, all grown up, and grandkids too. It's been a few years since I saw them but they're still mine. And Henrietta's." Duke felt his face heating up.

"And you want them to find out after the fact how you faded away for all those years when they never bothered to visit you in the nursing home that they paid for? Find out that you finally croaked on a bed that stunk like urine? Kick up your heels, Duke, while you can still lift a leg. Put your death in the news!"

Duke frowned and rubbed his chin. "I do get Christmas cards."

"And I'm sure they're personalized."

"Sometimes I get a snapshot of the grandkids."

"Sorry I hit the sore spot, but I've had a lot of practice." Kyle leaned across the table. "Look Duke, you should get a mission. A dangerous mission that you think is worth your life, which *you* think is fading—I didn't say it. But eventually it does come around to everyone, no exceptions. And you should do it before you start repeating *ah there's the spark* every third sentence, and before your tremor creeps into your legs and lands you on the urine mattress for good." Kyle's face looked honest and earnest. Duke tried hard to find another *just kidding* in it.

"So what are you getting at?"

"It's easy. Think of something you love so much that you would die to save it. Or something you hate so much that you would die to kill it. And make sure people hear about your final act, so your grandkids will know the story and tell it to their grandkids and on and on."

Duke stared at Kyle's face and tried to figure out what to read on it.

"TV's okay," said Kyle, "but you have to have it in print, too, so they can make photocopies. And some still shots just as you're doing the final act would be a good idea. Maybe you should hire a photographer for the critical moment."

Duke shifted in his chair. "Slow down a minute, Kyle. I'm...that's not exactly what I had in mind. You're getting way ahead of me."

"Look, I'm not the one who's suicidal. I'm just trying to help you out of your predicament. And Henrietta would be proud of you."

Duke was quiet for a long time. The repeating refrain of the reggae in the background seemed to elongate the old man's muteness.

"Don't you love something or hate something that much?" Kyle asked, his face solemn.

"You sound like a recruiter for suicide bombings."

"And I'm wondering if I have any material here to work with."

Duke took a deep breath. "I'm not a religious man, so it's hard to hate something. Love, yeah, sure. That was Henrietta. It *is* Henrietta."

Kyle reached across the table and grabbed Duke's bony shoulders and shook him. "Concentrate on hate! It's more reliable. Who or what do you *truly hate*?"

"Well." The cloud on Duke's face cleared away. "Well, I hate my best friend who made a pass at Henrietta when I was out of town. Forty years ago, or more. My ex-best friend."

"Uh, Duke, that rates a ho-hum and a so what." Kyle rolled his eyes. "Knocking him off will get you a column inch about a deranged grandfather, something your kids will never show to your great-grandkids. Duke, you're buying the beers, so I have to say it. You're not thinking *big*."

"He's already dead, anyway. My ex-friend. Diabetes. I didn't go to the funeral."

"Don't you read the papers? There's plenty to hate," Kyle said. "All those industrialists destroying whales. All those murderous dictators. All those drug lords polluting young lives for profit. All those pedophiles. All those lying politicians. All those hypocritical church-going racists and gay bashers and wife beaters."

Duke was caught midway into a long sip. He swallowed hard to keep it from coming back up.

Kyle's wide eyes narrowed into nickel slots. He exhaled slowly. "You beat your wife, didn't you." It was a statement.

Duke put the beer down with his trembling hand. He wagged his head to say no. He wished . . . he wished he hadn't drunk so much beer. He felt the weight of his jowls as he nodded yes. "It was a long time ago. When we were young. I hate myself for it."

Kyle let it sink in, more for Duke than for himself. He saw the wetness in the old man's eyes and said, "Those are

long-ago tears. Take them back. I know you loved her."
Duke's eyes got wetter and the moisture dripped out of
them onto the bags of skin below. He rubbed the bags and
the eyes and they were all red when he looked up at Kyle.

"At least you have one," Kyle said.

"Have what?"

"The family thing."

"Everybody's got family, except orphans. You an
orphan?"

Kyle waved a hand in the air as if he were asking to
be called upon in a grade school classroom. "Yes! I'm an
orphan, I'm an orphan!"

"Well, that makes me very sad. But you turned out
so well. I mean—you're the guy I've put trust in for my
future. Okay, it's my last hurrah before I'm over the edge.
But it's a kind of future." Duke scratched the back of his
neck. "So you're an orphan. No. You're not an orphan.
I see it in your eyes."

"Depends on your definition."

"Don't play hard to get with me, Kyle."

Kyle felt a tug, like a fishhook had caught him in
the stomach.

"So they cut you off," Duke said, "because you're
into men."

Kyle felt the yank beneath his diaphragm again and
hunched to pull the beer mug to his lips.

"Well?" Duke pressed.

"They're conservative folks. From the heartland. Not too far from here."

"Well, damn, they should love you." Duke reached across and squeezed Kyle's hand.

"Well, damn," Kyle said.

★   ★   ★

Three weeks passed before they met again. Duke had gone to the pub five nights in a row, and each time the bartender replied that he hadn't seen Kyle for a good long while.

When the younger man finally showed up, Duke wasted no time and pulled a sheaf of newspaper articles from his coat. He laid them on the table, all neatly clipped.

"There's a lot that I...I get mad about."

"Mad is not enough. *Hate.* Sorry to get down to brass tacks so fast." Kyle scanned the collection of headlines.

"Fast is okay. You know an old man like me doesn't have much time." Duke coughed when he tried to laugh.

"Ah, Duke, there's the...."

"Don't say it! A spark is not enough. It's gotta be bigger." Duke leaned forward and winked. "I may be old, but I can still pick up a thing or two." He spread the newspaper clippings between the beer mugs. "Okay, I hate the suicide bombers. Killing all those innocent folks just because they're trying to make a point. I hate the haters."

"Good as far as it goes, old man. But be practical," Kyle said. "If you knock out a suicide bomber for global credit, you have to destroy him before he blows himself up. And if he doesn't blow up and murder dozens, you won't get credit for anything big. It's a catch-22." Kyle tilted his head back and looked at the pressed-tin ceiling. "Let's go back to what you said—hating the haters. And focus on the big dogs who pay others to drive the car bombs and obliterate themselves. Think bigger."

Duke rubbed his knuckles across the table. "I suppose it's like in the war," he finally said. "You could shoot the little nobodies across the river that you spotted in your scope, who would have killed you, but it wouldn't add up to much either way."

"Wait, Duke. *You* were shooting people and *I'm* talking to *you* as if you were a newcomer at this?"

"Stupid young puppets," Duke said. "That's what we were, and that's what they need in a war. Same old story. I'm not saying *you're* a puppet. You're more like a puppeteer. Makes me feel younger. Usually the puppeteers are the older ones."

"A veteran," Kyle said, smiling. "Maybe I *am* working with some good material here. Don't worry, I won't ask how many Germans you killed."

"Koreans. I was killing Koreans. You want to put me in the grave earlier than I deserve?" Duke spilled foam onto the newspaper articles as he lifted his mug.

"What else do you have to show me?" Kyle pulled at the wet mat of newsprint. He peeled the layers apart until he saw a photo of a man with a big mop of hair; a large scrawl of words was penned in the margins. Kyle read the headline out loud. "Radovan Kara...Karaduzik again eludes capture by NATO."

"It's Kara-*dzitch*. Radovan Karadzic."

"Okay, yeah, I recognize the crazy hairdo, the smirk too. The Yugoslav guy who bombed Sarajevo to bits." Kyle's eyes tracked the article. "And they haven't caught the bastard yet? Now that's a guy I could hate."

"If you ever read the papers!" Duke grabbed the damp clipping and shook it in Kyle's face. "This monster blasted Sarajevo and even pointed the guns at the national library. Burned up every last book. Raped my homeland! Massacred thousands. Mass graves. All his doing."

"Homeland?" Kyle raised an eyebrow. "But you're from here, Duke. Chicago."

"My old man was from Yugoslavia. Okay, he was Serb, like this bastard, but born in the Bosnia part. Just being a Serb doesn't give you a permit to murder all those people." Duke clenched his fist.

"I suppose that just being *anybody* doesn't give you a permit to murder lots of people, right?" Kyle's face became somber. Then he grinned. "It sounds like you really hate this guy."

"Gave a bad name to my home country, on top of it all."

"You been there?"

"No. But I feel like I have. My old man told me stories. Taught me to talk Serb. And this Karadzic prick is a psychiatrist to boot."

Kyle spread out the clipping. "And the psychiatrist thing?" He straightened one edge of the paper until it tore where the beer had seeped in.

"They're all devious," said Duke. "Always trying to twist your thoughts."

"Sounds like you have experience, Duke." As Kyle reached for the piece with the photo, Duke clapped his hand down on the table.

"The man's a demon! A mass murderer! Eight years on the lam and no one's got the balls to find him and turn him in." Duke's right hand was shaking violently. He hid it beneath the table.

Kyle didn't know whether to add to the fire or douse it. He searched Duke's face, which was raised in defiance. "It looks like you have your man," Kyle finally said.

Duke straightened his back and gripped both edges of the tabletop. "I've picked my target and the time is now. I've got the travel agent looking for a cheap ticket. I bought the maps."

"Hey, wait. You said it was my call to say when you were losing your marbles and it was time to do the deed. And you're not losing them yet. If anything you seem younger tonight, with all that rage like a rod up your butt. You on any new medicines?"

"Shush, Kyle. Just the same old blood-pressure pills." Duke leaned over the table. "And you know what we're both thinking. If we wait till I'm loopy it'll be too late to get this thing done. A thing that all civilized men and women and mothers and fathers who have any idea of justice—they all know it's got to happen. If only there was one brave man."

"And don't forget the press, the photographers...," Kyle caught himself. "I'm not agreeing that the time is right. You've got more tread left on your tires and it's fuckin' dangerous what you're scheming."

"Don't curse. Henrietta wouldn't have it."

"But half of NATO has been chasing the guy for years. SWAT types in armored vehicles, tanks, fancy guns, intelligence operatives, payoffs...."

"All a goddamn...," Duke took a deep breath. "A toe-stubbing bureaucracy. And let me tell you, you're talking to a postal worker retiree. Expert in bureaucracy. Bureaucracy leaves a thousand holes open. And I'm ex-army. Danger? I don't have the purple heart to slap down in front of you, but it was close. Close more than once."

"You have me worried, Duke. I feel like I pushed you into this." Kyle downed another slug of beer but kept his eyes on the old man. Over the rim of the mug he said, "Of course there's the other timing issue. And I know you know what we are both thinking."

"That the NATO boys will get him first."

"A good thing, right?"

Duke's hands were back on the edges of the table, gripping it like a steering wheel. "And rob me of this, this sacrifice for my country?"

"You mean you want to be *the one*, for personal glory."

"You chicken-legged fairies! Prancing all over patriotism. No idea of sacrifice, noble causes."

Kyle knew Duke was ahead on the beers because he had been counting. "Slow down, Quixote." He reached across and patted Duke's knobby fingers. "And just where does patriotism get into the act? Serbia a province of America now? Maybe this is getting out of hand."

Duke looked around at the little neon beer signs and mounted hockey sticks and backlit bottles of amber booze beneath the American flag and the placard that said WRITE CHECKS TO YOUR POOR MOTHER, NOT US. "Kyle," he said, "Henrietta was a damn good mother and yesterday I put flowers on her grave with a note about what I'm up to and why, so it's all signed and sealed. Stop being a crybaby."

★   ★   ★

Kyle's new snakeskin cowboy boots clomped on the floor as he approached Duke. He sat at the table.

"You sure?" Kyle put his hand on Duke's wrist.

"Signed and sealed, just like I said last time. Leaving day after tomorrow." Duke fumbled his hand until it grasped Kyle's. "Bridge is burned. Shell's in the air. That's what we said at Inchon."

Kyle raised his cold beer mug and pressed it against Duke's left cheek, then drank half the pint.

"A toast to the dead?" Duke said, his jaw tight beneath the white stubble.

"Not yet. I'd say you're still alive enough to operate these." Kyle placed a silvery digital camera and a thumb-sized plastic device on the table.

"I know what the camera is, but what's this other thing?"

"A voice recorder. A tape recorder. But no tape, just this little memory chip." Kyle pressed his thumbnail against the base of the recorder and showed Duke the blue plastic strip that popped out. "When's the last time you ever wrote a postcard?"

"When I was in Ohio. I didn't want Henrietta to be worried about me. Or worried about what I was up to, which was no good. Maybe forty years ago."

133

"This'll be easier. You can tell *me* what you're up to, if you're okay, or in prison, or maybe worse. Press this button and talk, say whatever you want, put that sandpaper voice of yours into electrons. This end goes toward your mouth." Kyle handed it over. "Say something."

Duke put it against his lips.

"Not so close."

Duke's shaky right thumb pushed the *Rec* button. "Well, um, this is Duke. Sitting here with my friend Kyle. He looks skinnier every time I see him. Must be the fashion. He's a good guy. I'm ... I'm lucky to have him to talk to. Like a son or a grandson. Keeps me kickin'. No urine bed for me. I'm Duke from Chicago. And I don't know when I'll see him again ... my friend, my good friend, Kyle ...."

"That's enough." Kyle took the recorder. "Want me to play it back?'

"No."

Kyle pushed the *Play* button anyway and put the recorder to Duke's ear. Halfway through the playback Duke said "yeah, enough" and pushed it away.

"It's easy. Just press and talk. Then send me the little piece of plastic."

"Easy in a way. Never heard my voice before." Duke took the device from Kyle's hand and rolled it in his shaky palm.

Outside the pub Duke hugged Kyle and patted his back brusquely, then he squeezed him with all his force. Kyle stood awkwardly for a moment, took a deep breath, and hugged him back. Duke's stubble bit into Kyle's face.

"Kyle, don't worry. I've got no life anyway, except you." Duke pushed away from the hug and grimaced. "I bet you don't think I can do it, right? But I've got something, Kyle, I've got your stinger in here." He jabbed a finger at his own skull. "Gonna do something with the last of my worthless life."

Kyle shoved his hands into the front pockets of his jeans. "Just remember," he said, "you don't have to kill him. Just turn him in. Then come back and buy me a few more beers, if you want to."

They turned away from each other and Duke hid the tears in his eyes by ducking his head as they parted. Kyle walked a few paces away and turned back to Duke. "I hope you get him. I want to see you in the news."

★ ★ ★

Kyle, it's Duke here. How much time do I have on this gadget you gave me? It's Duke here, anyway, talking to you from greater Serbia. What day is this? June 7th. Doesn't matter. Think I'm some kind of reporter?

135

I'm working the trail. I'm in Pah-lay town, just up the road a few miles from good ol' Sarajevo. This is where they all said my target was holding out, so I thought I'd start tracking the rumors. I'm dressing like the old men here. Not the high fashion I'm used to. Ha ha. Got a cap on the bald top. Makes me look younger, so to balance that out I don't shave much. Keep the tottering old dope disguise, you know. Damn pretty up here in the hills, all the forests. My old man was right, rest his soul. It's a beautiful country.

You know my line, Kyle? I'm an old Serb returned from America to serve Doctor Karadzic, the savior of the Serb race. Or at least kiss his feet and offer all my savings to help with his protection. God, I've got a lot of cash on me. Money pouches in my armpit, my belt, even around an ankle. Somewhere else, too, but I can't remember where. You'll have to buy your beers on your own now. Maybe there's another guy. I'm not jealous. Really. Is there?

The cash. So far I'm not paying for lowdown. When you pay, you get tricky looks or made-up bullshit. Better to serve up the fanatic mumbo jumbo—we Serbs are the perfect race destined to FINALLY control our homeland. Reclaim what the Turks stole as they raped our women a few hundred years ago, or whenever it was. Surprising how so many of the folks here have dark hair. All that Turkish infiltration. But a lot of beautiful women. And strong, tall men! Just looking out for you, Kyle. You laughing now?

*So, my back hurts. All this hunching over and faking a limp.
You'd be proud of me. Chummed up with a taxi driver, gave him
my lines. And you know what? He's ex-militia, Serb militia
in Bosnia. Bragging about all the Muslims he whacked. And
I laid on him I'd killed a man or two in Korea, maybe more.
And that I would, you know, for the cause I'd . . . no question,
leading him on like that. Making like a brother, talking about
what rifle I like best, what kind of rounds. He ate it up, especially when I talked up how the heads exploded out the backside
when you were on the mark. You see it in the scope, if it's close
enough. You bet that set him off with stories. He's shot a hell
of a lot more enemy than I have. And I believe him because he
got so excited, laughing and shouting like he was holding a gun
instead of the wheel, that he damn near drove us off the road.
Name is Zoran. Hilarious guy, especially after we've loaded on
a few brews. It's good here, the beer. Called KB. The K stands
for . . . . I'm wandering off the . . . . Wait, I've got it, what I was
going to say. So Zoran knows an ex-militia chief who has a girlfriend whose friend is a niece or some sort of relation to Doctor
K. You know how to say "bingo" in Serb?*

★   ★   ★

It's me again, Kyle. It's Duke. Make that Dragan. Decided
my old name's not so bad. Never told you? School kids teased
me and called me "dragon" and I didn't like it, so my old man

*called me Duke to get me to stop crying. So it's Dragan here.
Little tired. Been at it a week or more now, chasing around,
picking up tidbits. Couldn't tell you the names of all the little
towns I've been to.*

*That guy, name of Zoran. He turned out to be a real sicko.
And I said he was like a brother. He wanted to take me on a
night tour of the hills above ol' Sarajevo. Nice views, he said.
Okay, I said, and we drove down from the Serb side. Took
a lot of windy roads, to stay clear of the checkpoints. It's past
sundown and he stops on a road that looks down on a bunch
of houses. He's most of the way through a six-pack and pops
the trunk and he's got a big high-powered rifle, type I've never
seen before with a sight that would let you shoot the nose off the
moon and says let's have some target practice, pick a window.
They're all lit up yellow. Even without the sight I could see
people at dinner tables. Still got 20/20, old man like me. You
know that, Kyle?*

*He says they're re-settlers. Muslims come back after the
peace. He sucks on another beer and says you go first. Some
kind of test. I tell him he should go first. For Serbia he says and
slams the chamber shut. I could see the window he was aiming
at. Kids down there too. Fish in a barrel. I say no, let me go
first, at this range it'll be easy even for an old soldier like me,
even one with a shaky right hand. Old bastard like me won't
have many more good shots like this, blah blah. He gives in
and hands me the gun. Damn heavy, but it feels natural, feels
good. I can see it all through the sight, like I was there at the*

table about to bite into some chicken myself. Mother, father, an old lady, a boy, a girl. . . . Don't think for a moment. . . . Not me, Kyle. I was in my stance, with my elbows on the car roof. Zoran was breathing down my neck. I . . . I wobbled the rifle and fired three times quick. Wild shots off into the valley, like I was shooting birds. 'Course he grabbed me and said what a fucking worthless old man I was and I yelled back that I had a bad hand and he said with all the goddam noise we had to get the hell out of there.

It was close, Kyle. I almost lost my cookies. Makes me wonder if I'm really the man for this job.

★　★　★

Kyle. It's me. Couple of days after I dumped the psycho Zoran. Well, truth is the psycho dumped me, but I would have dumped him first if I'd had the chance. Murderer through and through, like he had to scratch an itch. I bet you know I've had that itch too. No fooling you, Kyle. Anyhow, I know where to find Doctor K's niece. That drunk chump Zoran rattled that much out even before he took me shooting.

I'm in a village they call Celebeetsee. Rented a room in an old widow's house. She had that sparkle in her eye soon as we met. 'Course I didn't want to turn off the charm completely, because I needed the room. No Holiday Inns around here. Not that she's bad looking for an old girl. Well, damn. She's banging on the door. Give me a minute. Back in a jiff.

★ ★ ★

Okay. Here again. She's a lovely dame, the widow, and pretty shrewd too. She got me to sit on the couch, a small couch but I won't call it a love seat. Didn't take her long to go for the smooch. I'm not complaining but I kept my wits, asking her to get me to the niece so I could have an audience—yeah I said that, audience—with the Doctor. And Kyle, all of that was between kisses. It's been a while but I was still thinking of Henrietta and wondering if she was looking in from somewhere and at the same time I was so focused on the mission, and I coaxed it out of the gal, and she agreed and just then she put her hand on the inside of my leg and I had to feel her up a little. Even the old gals here wear those flimsy summer dresses. And I've got some juice left in me, Kyle, I do! Anyway the long and short is she made a promise, and a promise is real around here, to get me in contact with the niece, and so I feel like James Bond doing what it takes with the women to make the mission work, and besides, Henrietta loved James Bond. Especially when that guy Connery did it and it always made me jealous and I'm getting mad about it right now even though that was fifty years ago and I can feel my pressure going up, which reminds me I didn't take my pill this morning. Damn. I'll get back to you, Kyle.

★ ★ ★

Kyle, Dragan here and I've got news. The niece likes me. Milanka's her name, Milanka. Yeah, I gave her my lines about wanting to kiss the ring of the Doctor, and how I was finally at home with my own race, a beautiful race I might add. Well, she agreed and then she said welcome home and she shook my hand and it lasted a bit of an extra long time and I swear it wasn't my doing, it was hers. But Kyle, Kyle! She was looking straight into my eyes. Stars in her eyes. Stars in mine too. I read that somewhere, in some book, but here, right then, I had it for real.

The widow was there when I met Milanka, and I could feel the jealousy oozing out of the old gal. Damn near had to give her the boot so Milanka and I could have a corner to ourselves. A Serb goddess, that's what she is, Kyle. Okay, she's not nearly as young as you. You jealous yet? But let's say a generation down from me. Damn, I wish I was a poet so I could paint you the full picture. That's it for now, Kyle. I'm getting a little drippy in the nose. Sentimental.

★　★　★

It's Dragan here. Don't know where I left off. Could've been a million years ago. A week maybe. Guess that's what happens when lightning strikes. She's so soft. Milanka, I mean. Tells me she was lost until she found me. Man of her life and won't I stay in Serbia to be with her. Truth is, Kyle, I'd be with her anywhere. Antarctica. I was worried when she took the cap off the old bald head but you know what she did? She rubbed it and smacked it with a kiss. I know what you're thinking, she's poor and has sugar daddy in her eyes, but it's more than that and what do you know about love? Sorry, Kyle. To be harsh. But this is real as real can be. I hope you have it like this some day. Don't worry, I'll be good to her. All the time. I swear I will.

★   ★   ★

Kyle. You won't believe it. I saw the Doctor today. Kissed his hand. Milanka and I are in Belgrade now, shacked up at the Hotel Moskva. She took me to him and she hugged him. The people here love him, call him a saint. I handed him a fat envelope, and I have to say, I felt a real presence, and I was thinking maybe he is a saint, after all. . . . Shows you how the people feel, devoted people like Milanka, that he can visit here, right in the capital, and nobody breathes a word about it.

I can't do it, Kyle. I can hear you talking inside my head, telling me to go out in a fairy tale flash. Pushing me even though you only half meant it. I'm thinking that all along you were of two minds, two contrary minds, like Henrietta used to say. Pushing and pulling. And Henrietta would be proud of me, you said. Were you having some fun with me, seeing how far you could push me? That's okay, Kyle, you were just testing your talents. Like we all do when we're young. Doing me a favor without knowing it. It was your call. Joke's on you, sort of.

I can't do it, Kyle. But Kyle . . . you can do it. I'm sending this chip thing by overnight mail. It'll be there in two days, maybe one. Make the calls, alert the NATO boys, tell 'em where to find him. I didn't catch a number, but it's an old apartment block, third floor, on a little street called . . . called Bregalnova. B-R-E-G-A-L-N-O-V-A, two blocks down from the big road, Kralja Aleksandra. K-R-A-L-J-A A-L-E-K-S-A-N-D-R-A. It's right across from the church. And get a photographer if you want, but it's got to be fast because the Doctor moves around a lot. By the time you get this Milanka and I will be cleared out. Suppose I should thank you for all this. Maybe later I won't. I don't know, it's all kind of crazy. But Kyle? Thanks. You can do it. You can.

★   ★   ★

The male nurse felt Kyle's quivering fingers relax. Together, their two hands grasping the recorder slid from Kyle's ear onto the pillow near his chin.

"Is the message over?" the nurse asked.

The weak nod of Kyle's head left his mouth open and drooling. The nurse lifted the recorder from Kyle's fingers and placed it on the bed, just beyond the ridges of Kyle's folded legs. He gently wiped away the drool with a tissue as Kyle moaned, his tucked body vibrating beneath the sheet.

The nurse looked at his watch and injected more morphine into the intravenous line. He put his hand on

143

the bony prominence of Kyle's shoulder and stroked it lightly, thinking how all the ones with pancreatic cancer ended up small and baby-like.

The night-shift resident picked up the clipboard from the slot at the end of the bed. "How's he doing?"

"Lots of pain. But he just listened to a recording from a friend. I guess it's from a friend, or family."

"Canc in the panc," said the resident. "It always goes fast." Through the rising tide of bliss in his blood, Kyle could still hear. "He's too young for it. Should've happened to an older man."

A smile formed in Kyle's mind but never quite made it to his lips.

SUBMARINER

"Do you know there's zero ambient light down at seven hundred feet? I've got an external lamp on the hatch that I can rotate from inside. Hard to find a lamp that can take that kind of pressure. Had to make the servo rig for it myself." Fish looked up to see if the sunburned tourist with the buoy-shaped belly was still listening. The two faux blondes next to them at the bar had no interest in the minutiae of flow meters and ballast valves, and Fish had seen the way they rolled their eyes.

"So you are here testing your submarine because the law is easy and you can pay off whoever." Fish's drinking companion wiped away the beer that was dripping down one side of his speckled beard. "You Americans, always looking for an angle."

"Nah," said Fish. "It's the drop-off. The wall. A half mile out from the island, the sea drops thousands of feet. Edge of the Cayman Trench. You know how far offshore from Florida you'd have to go to get that kinda depth? Mid-Atlantic. Here we got the wall. That's why I brought her here—the smallest two-man sub in the world."

"You look too young to be captain of a submarine. Pulling my leg, are you?" The Swiss man smiled at one of the blondes, who looked away.

"I cut the first steel for *Adeline* when I was fifteen," Fish said flatly.

The man snorted. "You named it *Adeline*?"

"Yeah—that's the name of the girl they saved in a book I read when I was a kid. She was held captive in a chamber way down in Lake Winnetonka, and the only way they had to save her was to build a sub and pull her out, at night, when Mr. Evil was on land." Fish rested his lean frame on his elbows against the bar and rubbed one bare shin against the other.

"And Fish—did you make that up?"

"Fisher's my *last* name. People've called me Fish forever. Yours, again?"

"Stefan." Stefan wiped his beard a second time and smiled at two chattering brunettes in tank tops who had just arrived. One of the women smiled back. "And what do your parents think about you, here, a crazy boy with a submarine?"

"They're out of the picture. She, my mom, used to say I'm better with machines than people. We didn't get along so well. My dad? Who knows. Anyway, I'm adjusting the CO_2 absorption rate right now. The specs for the absorbent matrix don't quite translate to the small volume of *Adeline,* and the air feed may be too close to the absorbent bed, sucking up the O_2. Yesterday I was down at three hundred feet and got a little woozy. But it'll be fixed. On that dive I saw a sea lily that's never been described before, at least not in my books. I get the O_2–CO_2 worked out and I'll be down to seven hundred feet. That's where I hit pressure max for the design." Maneuvering the sub just next to the undersea cliff was no big trick, Fish continued, but nudging rare shells off the rocks and trapping them in a net at the front of *Adeline* took a lot of practice. "It's worth it, though. A shell like that can go for two, three thousand. Collectors around the world. Genus *Adansonianus.* I'll be going deeper to get more, once I'm past the CO_2 problem. I sell enough of those shells, I'll build the next sub and go even deeper."

There was a long silence after Fish had stopped talking. Stefan tore his gaze away from the woman who had smiled back and asked Fish how old he was.

"Twenty-three. But I've been at it awhile. I made the armrests for *Adeline* out of mahogany in shop class. High school. 'Course, to mount them on the inside of the hull, you can't just drill into the steel. That would bring down the compressive strength. You have to weld-mount them."

"What about girls around here?"

"Well, there's some with the cruise ships. I hate it when they come in. The locusts swarm over the best beach and leave their plastic cups all around. But when the sub's ready, they'll pay top dollar for a ride. And then there are the divers and the backpackers always coming through. A lot of pretty ones. We don't have that much to talk about." Fish was rubbing his thumb across a puddle of foam on the bar. "But there's this Venezuelan girl on one of the sailboats anchored out there. We get by with half-Spanish/half-English. Really sweet. She wants to go down with me in *Adeline*, but Rolf won't let her. Rolf's her husband. From Hamburg. He's about thirty years older. Nice guy. Sails all over the world, he says."

"So, you get any from her?"

Fish kept his eyes on the bar. "It's not like that, but sometimes I think . . . . And she's married and all that. But Rolf doesn't go onshore much. Likes his boat. Nice boat. Must have cost him a lot. Likes the sea, like me. Funny thing is Sylvia doesn't speak German, and he doesn't speak Spanish, and he doesn't know more than a few sentences of English, so they have to get by on just her half-English."

"So, is she on shore tonight?"

"Nah, I don't think so."

Stefan persisted. "Where does she go when she's on shore? Ripples?"

"Nah, she doesn't like bars. Sometimes she'll stop by here 'cause Toby's a friend of mine; guess he's taking a break tonight." Fish sniffed and looked toward a stretch of beach where several local boatmen were passing around a brown bottle and lighting a fire on the sand.

Stefan sniffed the air, too, and frowned. "*Scheiss.* What the hell is that?"

"It's the septic tank over there next to Maria's joint. About half the town's shit goes there and it backs up. And if the breeze turns our way.... Tank's too close to the water, too, so it's leaking into the sea. Wasn't made for all the people coming here now. But it keeps the sandflies down. They don't like it either. I tried to tell the locals how to fix the mess, but they don't want to bother with it." Fish drained his mug and stepped back from the bar. "Gotta go. Sun's up early. Thanks for the beer." Stefan gave a thumbs-up, and Fish walked off into the darkness.

★　★　★

Over the next three days, Fish fixed the CO_2 absorption bed and made two dives down to five hundred feet to test it. For each dive, *Adeline* had to be towed out of the cove to deep water and then back because the trip would take too long if Fish relied only on her tiny propellers. The first dive was fast and perfunctory, since he was focused on hitting the depth goal and making

149

sure his breathing was normal. He barely took time to look around.

For the second dive, the surface was choppy on the way out, and the forty-foot towline sliced in and out of the water as it snapped taut, then relaxed. Once out of the cove, an irregular wave sloshed into the hatch just as Fish closed it. The splash was a shock but also a relief in the heat, which became even more oppressive once the hatch was sealed and the fuselage was still bobbing on the surface, absorbing the rays of the high sun.

Fish twisted the buoyancy valves and put the sub into a spiraling dive. The air inside cooled quickly as he passed through the thermoclines, and the brilliant blue light flickering through the fist-thick portholes faded into a gray sameness. He aimed the sub toward the wall.

The great undersea cliff was dusted in sediment that had rested in place for hundreds or thousands of years, undisturbed even by the hurricanes, like the one that had blown through the year before. Fish scanned the ledges of the cliff face for the rare anemones he'd seen on an earlier dive. He told himself that if Sylvia were here, he would joke and say, "I call them *Sylvianamarinus*, in honor of you." And she would laugh with that light bell peal he had heard when they first met on the pier and she had thought it funny that he had his own submarine.

★　★　★

The air was heavy and hot the next afternoon when Fish passed by Toby's café.

"Halloo, submariner!" yelled Stefan from a table behind a hibiscus bush. Big Toby was there, too, his plastic chair ready to collapse. His beefy black arms were folded across an apron that was bright white except for the greasy patch that always rubbed against the grill. Stefan had a girl next to him and several glasses of beer in front of him. "Sit, sit, my underwater friend," he said with a careless wave of his hand. "Come hear about the hurricane."

Fish smiled briefly and slid into a chair. The smell of frying onions and fritters made his stomach rumble.

"So, before the hurricane," Toby continued, nodding at Fish, "it was getting worse and worse around here. A lot of folks were jealous of my business, growing like it was, and jealous of the stream of tourists, thinking what money I must be making. A couple of mornings I found notes tacked on the kitchen door, nasty stuff. One night I chased a man from my house, and I found a can of gasoline tipped on the porch. I had to start sleeping with a gun."

"But what about the *hurricane*?" bellowed Stefan.

"It came three days later. Folks talk about the big tragedy. All the houses that got knocked down. All the wrecked business. All the tourists gone. But I wish that hurricane had swept everything away. Everything." Toby swooped his arm through the air as if to clear the table in one broad stroke. His bald head was beaded with sweat. "Then maybe we could all shake hands and lose our greed and envy and start from zero. Be nice to each other again. But we weren't so lucky."

"Well, I'm glad you're back in business," said Stefan as he raised a glass and tilted the beer into his gullet. He burped and said, "You, Fish the Fish-man. Why so quiet?"

"I was down all night."

"Down where?" said the girl next to Stefan. She had an American accent.

"In *Adeline*."

The girl shrieked with laughter. "All night? She must have been good!"

Stefan swallowed more beer. "That's not a woman, it's his sub. What do you mean you were at it all night?"

"Night dive. Five hundred feet. Bull sharks. A school of tuna as big as a cloud, all around me. Squid. And a worm-like thing, the size of a human. I bet no one has seen it before. Had to wait till sunrise to come up. For the towboat to pick me up. Had to load extra O_2. A little cold too. But the human worm. He was thick and he pulsated; the feathery things along his body, I mean. He came right up to *Adeline* and—"

"Okay, so you didn't get laid last night," said Stefan as he turned his grin toward the American girl.

★　★　★

The following afternoon Fish walked down the road and out onto the pier near where the yachts were anchored offshore. Sylvia had invited him to come to the boat. Fish could dive with Rolf for lobster. They could have dinner on the deck. Fish thought of asking if all of that was okay with Rolf, but didn't. He'd memorized the profile of her boat—her and Rolf's—and he saw her there waving. A lemon-colored scarf was tight around her chest, and a short floral sarong hung loosely from her hips. She hopped into the small Zodiac alongside the yacht and gunned the motor, swerving toward him in a broad arc, her thick, black hair lifting into the air behind her.

"Fish, *como estás?*"

"Okay, *que tal?*"

She kissed his cheek as he stepped down into the Zodiac, which rocked and tipped Fish off balance. His hand hit her hip as he tried to steady himself, and it rested there for a second as Sylvia grabbed his arm and said, "Easy to fall—such a little boat."

She was light on the throttle as they puttered back to the yacht. Fish could feel the sweat beading on his face. He told her about all the adjustments he'd made to *Adeline* and about his night dive and the giant worm. Sylvia laughed and let her hand brush against his. She said, as far as Fish understood her Spanish, that he was like a new Magellan.

From a distance her husband had the fit body of a younger man, but as Rolf stepped onto the Zodiac, Fish was reminded of his leathery skin and the gray hairs in tufts behind his ears. Rolf studied Fish's face through wire-rim spectacles that magnified his eyes, then he spoke a few words to Sylvia and pointed to indicate that they would dive for lobster at a coral shoal not far away.

Rolf was swift in the water, and in a few minutes, at a depth of twenty feet, he was gesturing toward a spiny lobster so that Fish could see it beneath an overhang. Rolf jabbed his gloved hand and grabbed it. Fish was out of air and came up. A few seconds later Rolf was on the surface, the lobster whipping its tail in the German's webbed sack. As the two men treaded water, Rolf said, "Fast, you must be . . . and go like . . . ." He chopped his free arm into the water. "Then is he yours."

Rolf caught two more lobsters, each time poking Fish's shoulder and pointing to the prey before he snatched it. Each time, Fish was out of air and came up first.

Sylvia hovered nearby in the Zodiac until Rolf climbed aboard so she could take him and their catch back to the yacht. She returned to where Fish was plunging down to study a coral outcropping that flashed with the bold colors of the creatures that lived and died without ever leaving their craggy clump. Fish rose and floated belly-up on the water, his arms outstretched beneath the tamed, low sun.

"*Todavía no he nadado*," Sylvia said as she eased the rubber boat up to Fish. "Rolf makes the lobster. Let's swim." She took off the colored veils that covered her bikini and jumped in. He stared at her through his mask as she wriggled downward, encased in blue. Fish felt his heart stop in mid beat. He swam to catch up, timing his strokes to glide on top of her. Sylvia locked her legs around him, and they slowly rose through their bubbles. He clunked his mask into hers when he tried to kiss her at the surface, and Sylvia laughed a tinkling laugh, like seashells dropping on pebbles.

When the sun hit the horizon they swam to the drifting Zodiac and laughed about the awkward tugging and pulling that was needed to climb up and over the side. They let their hands touch as Sylvia steered them back to the yacht.

Rolf already had the dinner laid out topside. He shook his head impatiently when he saw Fish crack open his lobster. "No, this way." He wrenched apart another carapace, then meticulously plucked the flesh from its deepest creases. "Is better. To get the meat."

With Sylvia's help and his own few words of English, Rolf asked how deep and how far Fish could go in the sub, what swell height he could manage when on the surface, how fast the sub could go. Rolf had no interest in the strange life-forms that Fish said could be seen down deep, but they made Sylvia's eyes light up.

Fish was licking a finger cut by a lobster spine when he looked up and saw Rolf staring directly at him with a wide, stationary smile.

"Sylvia likes sub. You take her," said Rolf.

Sylvia put her hand on her husband's arm and said, "*Gracias, gracias,* Rolf," shaking her wild hair and grinning. She kissed him on his unshaven cheek.

Rolf pointed at the dismantled radar gear scattered around the base of the mast and moved his hands as if to show a job to be done. He set to work while Sylvia and Fish carried the dishes below. After they'd washed the plates, the two sat across from each other at the cabin table as Rolf's footsteps and tools sounded above them.

"I have pictures, Fish." Sylvia reached for an album and showed him photos of her family and the pink clapboard house where she grew up on a dirt street in the coastal town of Cumaná. There were shots of Sylvia in a neighborhood fashion show, parading past tinsel and plastic flowers in translucent blouses, high heels, and slit skirts. Sylvia slid a bare foot over Fish's and pressed. He asked polite questions about the pictures and her family as their feet caressed and retreated beneath the table. Fish occasionally glanced up to the narrow window panels above a bookshelf, through which he could see Rolf's calves intermittently passing by.

"Sylvia, maybe we've been down here long enough." Fish was starting to stand when Sylvia reached across the table and squeezed his hand; he retracted his arm by reflex. "Sorry, I.... With him up there...." Fish looked away.

Rolf's back was toward them as they climbed up the ladder from the cabin. When Sylvia asked if she could take Fish back to shore, he nodded without turning. "*Gute Nacht*."

When they reached the pier, Fish stood and held on to the dock. "Thanks for showing me the pictures," he said.

Sylvia reached up to put a hand on each of Fish's shoulders. He looked toward the rocking lights of the yacht and squeezed her with one arm. Sylvia stood on the tips of her toes and nudged her cheek against his. They kissed, kissed again, and he turned toward the ladder to climb up on the pier.

"When do we go in *Adeline*?"

"Tomorrow is okay, if the weather is good. See you at Toby's at noon." Fish gave a quick wave as she gunned the throttle, looking back at him. He could just make out Rolf's back, hunched beneath a floodlight hanging from the mast.

★　★　★

The next day Fish was up at sunrise, testing compressed air tanks on the dock next to the hoist from which *Adeline* was suspended, compact and heavy, just above the surface of the water. The sea was as smooth as a ray's wing, undulating gently.

He heard steps on the dock, looked up, and stopped whistling. It was Propface. He never objected to the nickname he'd gotten after having his face shredded by the back end of one of the wooden water taxis that careened along the coast. He used to dive for conch, but he didn't bother with the sea anymore.

He was drunk. "So, Mista Bottom, you goin' down oh up today?"

"Well, this isn't a helicopter hanging here, so I guess I'm going down." Fish kept himself busy with the tanks.

"You makin' any *cambio* w'dat yellow monsta yet?"

"Not much yet. I gotta work out a few things first. It'll come," said Fish.

Propface sat down cross-legged and teetered. "Ders plendi *cambio* out there. Jus' gotta know who da talk to." Propface reached out for a line of tubing and started twisting it. "Your monsta's like dis tube. You put sumptin' in one end and it come oudda udder end and no one see it."

Fish turned his head and met Propface's bleary eyes. The man's nose was mostly missing, one cheekbone was caved in, and the matching eye socket was missing a brow. Several roughly parallel scars, thick and knotted, ran across his entire face. Fish knew the visage well enough that he didn't have to stare.

"Yora nice boy. No one dever know. Nice white boy. Jus' need to know who da talk to. Lotta stuff movin' in dis place."

"Propface, you look hungry. Here's some *cambio*. Go get some *pasteles* and take a snooze." Fish handed him some grimy bills.

Propface unbent his legs and stood up without taking the money. "Yora nice boy, Fish. Tanks. I'm okay widda *cambio*." He rose dizzily and leaned himself against a pylon. "See ya, Fish."

"See ya."

Propface was singing as he made his way back to the hard-packed dirt at the end of the dock. Fish put some new clamps on the joints between the tanks and the tubing, then went to meet Sylvia at Toby's. There was a slight onshore breeze, and sunlight was flaking off the sea beyond his right shoulder.

Big Toby was on his patio, stabbing his beefy hands toward the sky and shouting, "I don't know the man!" His body was shaking beneath his apron as the shadows of palm fronds played across his broad face. The skinny man in front of him was puzzling over a piece of paper in his hands. He wore a dull-blue jacket with an embroidered patch stitched on the left shoulder. Obviously from

159

the mainland, he was struggling with the English of the island. He said they'd stopped a boat, and the man on it had said something about Toby's café. The official attempted to describe the man again.

"I don't know him!" Toby grabbed the paper. The skinny man grabbed it back and started shouting in Spanish.

Fish put his hands in the pockets of his shorts and eased himself to a distant table. The skinny man left the patio with a glare and a curse.

Toby sat down next to Fish. "He wants something out of me. The bastards sniff and nose in anywhere they think there's money." Fish started to ask what the problem was but stopped when he saw Sylvia striding toward the gate, swinging her arms as if she were on a catwalk. The skinny man in blue looked her up and down as they passed each other.

"That girl is some magnet," said Toby. "She could pull down a freighter."

Fish walked out to meet her, trying to control his smile.

"*Que rico el día!*" Sylvia said as she unfurled her arms toward the sky, kissing Fish on both cheeks.

"Yep, a fine day. *Adeline* is ready," said Fish. "I fixed the lateral buoyancy tanks, but don't be surprised at the tilt when we start diving. We'll try four hundred feet.

There's a gap in the wall, maybe it's a cave. We'll give it a look. Oh, and thanks for dinner last night. How's Rolf?"

"He is good. But today is our day. You and me and *Adeline*." Sylvia grabbed Fish's arm and pressed her head against his shoulder.

They walked between shaded shacks surrounded by packed dirt and creeping sea grape. At the dock, bright-yellow *Adeline* was hanging from the hoist, her steel wings making her resemble a strange bird taking flight. Without the wings and two short towers, the sub would look like nothing more than a ten-foot sewer pipe capped at both ends.

Fish busied himself describing to Sylvia how she should slide feet-forward into the hatch tower in the middle of the fuselage, lie down in the body of the sub, and then shimmy backward to where she could sit upright in the rear tower—a cylindrical stub with three plexiglass ports at eye level. He would get in after her and sit with his head in the forward tower.

"There's enough room for your legs to fit around my back. I'll keep the hatch open while we get towed out. It'll be pretty hot until we're underwater," Fish said as he waved to a baseball-capped boy sitting in a nearby skiff that had a small motor strapped on the stern. Fish turned the winch to lower the sub onto the water, where she floated.

He held Sylvia's hand as she stepped onto one of the wings and leaned against the circle of the open hatch. She braced her arms and lifted both legs like a gymnast, extending them down into the hatch until she was standing in the sub. Fish untied the winch lines and readied the towrope, which he tossed out to the boy approaching in the boat.

"Okay, now slide in, and then back yourself up so you can sit. Don't touch any switches, okay?"

Sylvia's head soon appeared in the porthole of the rear tower. She was frowning but her face brightened when she saw Fish, and she blew him a kiss.

Fish lowered his legs into the open hatch and waved for the boy to tow them out. *Adeline*'s prow submerged and rose against the gentle waves as the towboat's outboard motor whined. It wasn't a minute before Sylvia was shouting.

"Fish! It's hot. *Demasiado.* I will sick!" She kicked her bare feet against his calves; he was still standing in the open hatch, his upper half in the light breeze.

"What?" Fish kneeled down to hear her. "Okay, come out." Fish lifted himself out of the hatch and Sylvia emerged, her delicate brown skin glistening with sweat. She was on the verge of crying.

"It's hot. I need *aire.* I cannot get *aire.*"

"The sun heats things up. I know it's small inside. Maybe you're a little seasick. It all goes away when we dive. It's cool down there. But maybe I should take you back."

"No, no, no, Fish. I want to go with you!" She pulled herself up to join him on the sub's hull and grabbed his arm. "*Podemos*...we can sit like this, on the top, and when we are out there, I go in again. Please! I want to stay with you." She moved closer and clung to him.

Fish patted her shoulder awkwardly and nodded. "Okay, sure. Stay on top for now. There's a fan inside. It'll blow on your face when we're ready to dive. Then it cools off."

A few minutes later, after they'd been towed to the deep water, Sylvia was still trembling as she squirmed back into *Adeline*, followed by Fish. He closed the hatch and turned the wheel above his head to make the seal. Sylvia's sweaty legs were around his hips.

Fish reached forward to turn several squeaky valves as the nose of the vessel tilted downward. "It'll be a little steep here," he said.

The sub tipped forward and the water splashed against the windows surrounding their faces. Soon the sub was nearly vertical, and Sylvia was sliding into Fish's back.

"Hold yourself against the armrests so you don't slide down," Fish instructed. She pushed her elbows against the polished mahogany of the armrests and eased her pelvis off of Fish's back. As their downward glide became more gradual, Sylvia shimmied to the rear and sat upright. Fish felt her shivering in the faint stream of air coming out of a plastic accordion tube.

"Once the sweat dries off, you'll be comfortable." Fish patted her bare foot, resting near his thigh. "We're at fifty feet now. The wall is in front of us, not too far. We'll hit it at a depth of one hundred feet and then make our way down the face. Before I added the electric propellers to *Adeline*, I had to do it all by gliding." Fish stopped talking and the sub was filled with the sound of their breathing. "D'you see how the light is fading? Look out the porthole. Don't worry, I have a light right here." Fish raised his hand to the hatch-mounted lamp.

A sudden hissing sound crescendoed into a mechanical scream.

"Fish! What is it?"

"Just a minute." He quickly folded his torso into the narrow fuselage and extended one arm, straining for the valves that controlled the air feed. His fingers clasped the correct one and turned. The screaming suddenly stopped. Sylvia was gasping behind him.

"Just a joint that popped loose. I switched the line to a different cylinder."

"It happens before?"

"No. First time."

They slid through the water soundlessly. To their left, Fish pointed out three crevices that sliced into the ageless great wall, a series of jagged rock edges falling vertically beyond sight. At four hundred feet he said, "That's a sea lily, you see it? That one only lives deep down. It has little legs beneath that umbrella of tentacles, so it can walk along the ledge. It's a walking plant." Fish swiveled the lamp to make sure Sylvia could see the creature.

"I see it," said Sylvia, "all alone. Alone with the rocks."

The top of the lily had white, feathery arms arching out in a perfect circle. The feathery spokes were supported by a long, crooked stem that branched at its bottom into irregular fingers resting on the narrow shelf of rock. If there had been the slightest current, it would have toppled over, drifting downward like a leaf in slow motion, its delicate bloom grazing the hard mineral edges and leaving its broken arms in a silent trail straight down to the bottom.

As they went deeper there was a creaking sound. Sylvia tapped her knee against Fish's hip to ask what it was.

"The specs on the plexiglass portholes go to seven hundred feet of pressure. But they groan a little as we go down. Don't worry about it. Look. Here are some spider crabs. Not so rare." Fish reached up to rotate the lamp. "D'you see? They're really small. You see?"

There was a soft pop, and the light went out, leaving them in darkness.

"Hmmm." Fish flipped the switch back and forth. "We lost the light." He pulled out a flashlight and pointed it through his porthole at the crabs with long legs as thin as needles. "See them?"

There was a bump as the front end of the sub gently hit the cliff face.

"Fish, now we go up? Is there *aire?*"

"Plenty of air in the tanks. But let's go to five hundred if it's okay with you. Just a little further. It's worth it." He reversed the propellers to ease them away from the cliff and put the sub into a shallow dive. The plexiglass creaked under the pressure again just as Fish said, "That's five hundred feet. We're there."

Sylvia reached forward and put her hands on Fish's shoulders. She pressed her shins against his hips.

"You are right. It is beautiful here, *capitán.*"

"I wish the big worm would come so you could see it. Maybe it's out there. But without the light . . . he can't see us. Maybe he can sense us anyway."

"How you know he is a he? Maybe a woman."

"It could be, or it could be both. A lot of these marine animals are sequential hermaphrodites, going from one state to the other depending on the environment."

"So you are *científico!*" Sylvia's laugh rang around the closed compartment.

Fish twisted the ballast valves, and they ascended in a slow, tilted spiral. "We have to go around and around like this to see what's above us, looking sidewise through the portholes. Some of the big dive boats up there have five-foot propellers. *Adeline* wouldn't like to bump into them."

The wind had risen by the time they reached the surface, and the sub bobbled with the cresting waves as spray hit the towers. The sky was blue except for a distant storm's gray edge that appeared and disappeared with the swell.

"It's a little rough," said Fish. "I'll look for the tug." He lifted himself out of the hatch. The boy in the baseball cap was a dark spot at the mouth of the cove hundreds of yards away. Fish yelled and waved as he gripped the fuselage between his knees.

"Fish. I get sick!" Sylvia yelled from within the steel chamber.

"He saw me. He's coming." Fish spoke into the open hatch. "If you have to puke...vomit, go ahead. We'll get you back as quick as we can."

Fish heard her retching as the boat boy sped toward them, bouncing hard on the choppy water. At a distance of fifteen yards, he eased off the throttle and threw the rope. It missed Fish. The boy tried and fell short again, and Fish reached out too far trying to grab it and toppled into the water. He stroked against the waves to grasp the rope and tied it to the sub's bow ring. As he tried to climb back on, a wave knocked him against the forward edge of one of the wings, which promptly rose into the air with the swell and nearly trapped his head when it slapped back down.

Fish heard Sylvia scream.

"Take us in! I'll stay in the water. Pull us in!" Fish gripped the rope where it was knotted to the nose of the sub and extended one arm high to motion toward the cove.

The rope tensed and the sub rotated into line with the skiff as it accelerated. The wind was onshore and *Adeline* rode the waves like a surfboard, tilting up in the rear and nose-diving into the troughs, each time submerging Fish for a moment. Fish clung to the rope with both hands, timing his breaths to the rising glide and downward plunge, and trying to ignore the sound of Sylvia screaming inside the fuselage.

Then a steep nosedive lasted too long. Fish was pressed deep into the frothing water as *Adeline*'s tail rose straight up on the crest of a large wave. When at last he returned to the surface, choking, his hands were still on the rope, but the sub had flipped over. The rope stayed tight and the inverted vessel swiveled around to follow the boat. Fish felt for the running rods along one of the wings and pulled himself underwater to look into Sylvia's porthole. For only an instant, through the watery blur, he saw an elbow. She was upside down. He had no way of knowing how much water had entered the open hatch when

it flipped; no way to tell if she was now doing a head-
stand in sea water. Fish pulled on the runner and thrust
his head up for air. He yelled to the boy to go as fast as
he could, and heard the motor's whine rise before he
went back down beneath the sub, probing with his free
hand for the hatch. He tried to pull himself in, but the
sub lurched, driving the rim of the hatch into his neck.

Fish pulled his head to the surface again, still holding
on to the runner with one hand as *Adeline* entered the
calmer waters of the cove. Again he plunged under the
sub. He got a hand around one of Sylvia's ankles, but the
water dragged hard against him and wrenched him from
the vessel. He wouldn't be able to get her out while it was
upside down. How much time had passed, would pass,
before they could get to the winch? When the pier was
close, he swam to it frantically and climbed up the ladder.

"Come here! Here!" he shouted to the boat boy. Fish
grabbed the cable clip, released the winch, and jumped
back into the water. He hooked the clip to the bow and
raced back onto the pier again, cranking the gears to
raise *Adeline*'s nose. After a moment of vertical suspen-
sion, like a yellow bird pointed to the sky, Fish released
the cable. *Adeline* slammed down on the water, upright.
Fish leaped from the pier and dove head first into the
hatch. He saw only Sylvia's brown legs in a layer of water.
He struggled to pull her body through the fuselage by

her knees, then her thighs, then her hips, until he had her face nose-to-nose with his. He dug his fingers into her shoulders and pulled her torso up through the hatch, then the rest of her. Her mouth was open as he laid her body out on the sub's wing and there was a rough gash at her hairline where her head had smashed into the steel when the sub flipped over. Fish breathed into her lungs furiously. He closed his eyes as he did so because it was unbearable to look at her expressionless face.

The water in the cove was now still. So was Sylvia. He turned her on her side and slapped her back repeatedly, then resumed mouth-to-mouth and pumped her heart.

No matter how many times he checked for a pulse, there was none.

Fish thought he should cry but he didn't. He stared at her delicate body and traced with his eyes the searing outline of her arms and fingers against the brilliant canary-yellow paint. Water droplets on her brown limbs were sparkling in the sunlight.

A long, whining whistle came from the shore beyond the pier. For the first time, Fish looked up. The boy in the baseball cap was gone. Propface was sitting in the shade of a dusty tamarind tree, staring at the trio at the end of the dock: Fish, Sylvia, and *Adeline.*

Now Fish let out a sob. He bent forward and pressed his face into the steel and moaned and rocked.

"Dat's okay, man. Dat's okay. Happens all da time roun' here. You tried. You tried. Ah tell 'em. Yeah, ah tell 'em you tried." Propface was now on the dock, holding on to the winch pole. "C'mon, man. Let's gedder up an' oudda here."

Fish raised his eyes toward the disfigured man. He lifted Sylvia onto his shoulder, then had no choice but to take the hand of Propface to get the load up and onto the dock. Once ashore he placed her on a tarp beneath the trees and covered her face with his T-shirt.

"Damn pretty girl. *Damn* pretty. You were almost lucky," Propface said, nodding. He seemed sober.

"I'll run to town. I'll get somebody. You'll watch her?"

Fish was three steps away when Propface said, "I'll take care of her. But no one know. Jus' you an' me. No need, you know."

Fish paused and turned his head back toward the water. He squinted, wondering how it was possible that he had arrived at this moment. Then he turned and ran, his bare feet thumping against the dusty earth toward town.

Big Toby wasn't at his café, so Fish darted into the dive shop next door and told the woman there to call the police cabin up the road to report an accident at the cove. "A bad one," he said. Because Sylvia wasn't a local, he knew there would be calls to the mainland. Then Fish was running again, to look for Rolf.

There was no other way to get out to the yacht, so he swam. He pulled himself up partway by a fender line and called out but there was no response. He swam to the stern and climbed up the ladder. There was no answer when he pounded on the locked cabin door. The yacht was battened down. The Zodiac was gone.

It was almost dusk when he returned to find the small crowd around the refrigerated meat locker where they had taken Sylvia. The silhouettes of huddled men were visible in the misted light from the solitary yellow bulb. Fish stepped into the hazy coolness and saw her naked body on a wooden pallet; it appeared as if someone had cut her clothes off. Three of the five men inside were kneeling next to her, talking and staring and moving her limbs.

"What the fuck are you doing? Get the fuck out!" Fish pushed one of the squatting men, toppling him backward. Two of the others grabbed Fish's arms and held him.

"Let him be, let him be," Big Toby boomed from the doorway. "Fish, we have some ohficials here."

Fish recognized the skinny one in the blue uniform who had been grilling Toby earlier in the day. There was another one, in a brown uniform, still squatting. He spoke English with a mainlander's Spanish accent. "Looks like the girl wasn't alone." He pulled up on one of her knees and pointed to a translucent ooze in a spot on the tarp beneath her labia.

Fish broke free and roared, "Leave her alone!"

"Fish." Toby was at his side, grabbing him in a bear hug. "Calm down. Where's her man? Calm down. Where is he?"

"He wasn't there. I went to the boat." Fish was struggling to breathe against Toby's tight hold. "To tell him."

There was a clatter of Spanish between the two uniformed men. Toby eased his grip on Fish. The squatting man let Sylvia's leg drop with a thud and stood.

"The German," said one of the other men huddled around the body. "My wife saw him go out in his rubber boat. Out to a big cruiser passing by. They took him on and went straight out."

"A *médico* comes in the morning," said the man in brown, glaring at Fish. "He'll take a look and tell me what is the truth. But first, you tell me. What is *your* story?"

Fish told them what had happened. He was shaking by the time he concluded, "There's the boat boy who pulled us in. And Propface. I left her with Propface. I ran. I ran to town."

"We have to keep you," said the man in brown, shrugging.

"I'll keep him," said Toby. "He won't go anywhere. Can't go anywhere."

The official in brown asked for two other men to take him out to Rolf's yacht. Toby took Fish to his home, laid him on a couch, and turned on the television.

Fish sipped the beer Toby poured for him but Propface's mutilation flashed in Fish's mind, and he retched. Toby was a dim, aproned mass going back and forth beyond the kitchen doorway.

Fish didn't know how long it had been when the two officials returned to the house and sniffed the simmering peppers and grouper. Toby dished it out for them as Fish watched from the couch. The overhead lights were out by then, and the foreheads of the two officers glowed blue in the television's flicker while they ate noisily.

"We found him," said the larger one, the boss.

"Her man?" asked Toby.

"The guy with the face. You call him Propface. He was floating belly down. Close to the yacht. He's even more banged up now." Sauce was dripping down the man's chin as Fish fixed his gaze on him. "No papers in the boat. We broke the lock. You had a busy day, good boy. Two people dead."

Fish felt bitter stomach juice on the back of his tongue. "I left him with her. He was alive, he was fine. He was watching her."

"Her man," said Toby, "he was in the business. Must've been. Else why would he leave like that?" Toby poured beers for the two visitors.

"A difficult situation. Very difficult," said the boss.

"Bad spot for such a good boy," said Toby.

The man in brown scooped a slug of grouper into

his mouth. "Very good you feed us. You're good in the kitchen. Lots of people like your table. The good boy— can he cook too?"

Toby answered by ladling out more sauce. Fish stared at the rising horizontal lines on the television screen; the fluttering reminded him of the rhythmic beating of the feathery edges of the giant deepwater worm.

"Can't imagine how he can cook much in that shack of a *casa* he lives in," said Toby. "Fish, you have some family you could call? Get a little help, maybe some cash?" Fish met Toby's eyes as the host leaned forward to pour more beer. Toby missed the rim of the mug, and beer dripped off the edge of the rattan coffee table onto the skinny man's trousers.

"*Puta madre!*" he snapped, glaring with red eyes.

The boss man laughed. "My friend here is a little rough." He patted the wet leg. "Doesn't know how to handle himself. A situation like this."

Fish sat upright. He was sweating. "It'll be tough to track her down. My mother. I'll try first thing in the morning."

The visitors kept drinking and Toby kept pouring. Fish gave up the couch for the men when Toby slapped a DVD into the video player. In a few seconds they were watching a porno movie.

"Fish, why don't you go lay your head down on my bed. You're not in the mood for this movie. You look sick." Toby waved his hand toward the narrow corridor next to the kitchen. "I think our friends are going to stay the night."

"*Sí, sí,* we'll see what you say in the morning... how good you cook something for us," said the man in charge, his eyes fixed on the screen.

Fish went into Toby's room and examined the window, wondering how much noise he would make if he crawled out. He paced along one wall until he noticed that he was making the floorboards creak and sat down on the bed. A poster of Louis Armstrong stared at him from the wall, with cheeks bulging out so far that they seemed about to pop.

Fish needed to pee and wanted to vomit. Despite the yelps and moans coming from the video, Toby must have heard Fish click open the door to the toilet, because he was there crowding the narrow space even before Fish could put his chin over the edge of the toilet bowl.

"Get up, Fish." It was a whisper. "Either you got a lot of cash or you have to get out. They'll take you over tomorrow. Things'll go worse on the mainland. They'll be trying to pin two dead ones on you. Double the price. A foreigner will have even less chance than a local. That's *no* chance. There's money under the lamp next to the bed. Don't say anything. Just get out. Time for me to pour for our friends." Toby's sweating hand grabbed Fish by the neck and pulled him up to his feet. Toby reached over Fish's shoulder to yank the flush string and then he was gone.

Fish found the dollars under the lamp and eased himself over the windowsill into the softly crackling palm fronds. He crouched as he made his way up the slope from the bungalow and followed a row of trees that shaded him from the moonlight and led him back to the edge of the road that would take him to *Adeline*. He skirted several open-air bars spilling out cheerful voices until finally the road was empty and dark as it curved toward the cove. Fish worried about Toby as he ran. And he calculated how far the remaining charged air canisters would take him.

The half-moon was lifting itself off the cusp of the hills as he slipped between the trees, picking his way between the plastic bottles and other trash scattered by the families living in the shacks farther up in the tangle of brush and sea grape near the cove. Just before stepping from the cover of the trees toward the shoreline and the dock, he heard a low whistle. His eyes finally found the faint outline of two bony legs stretched out on the ground.

"I knowed you lovin' her too much. Lovin' da monsta. Da yellow monsta."

Fish froze, then slowly stooped. He stared.

"Long day, Fish." Propface was lying on his back, his head resting on an empty milk carton. Fish tried to breathe several times before he got any air into his lungs.

"They said you were dead."

"They give me *cambio* 'nuf to lie low. And uh coupla smacks. Nodnuf to quit dis good 'n gracious life."

Fish looked around and knelt on all fours. "You fucking...piece of *shit*," he whispered. "They should've smashed your brains out."

"Wasin' me, Fish. Wasin' me. I godda tell yuh, wasin' me. They's the ones messed with her."

Fish crawled forward and grabbed Propface's arm. "You were supposed to watch her."

"Ah did watch her. Ah did watch dem. Budah couldn't myself. Couldn't."

Fish tasted the sourness of rising vomit and swallowed it back. "Tell me what's going on! Tell me. Where's Rolf?"

"Don' madder. She was gone from dis gracious life. Her old man was dun widder. He know da biznuss. Got his new boat and plendi *cambio*. He was on ta you an' her. He know da biznuss, movin' candy here an' der. Lodda friends. Yuh bedder go. Budah din't. Ah din't."

Fish hit him in the chest. "Tell them I didn't do it. Tell them it was an accident. Tell them Sylvia and I were...." Fish lunged on top of Propface and grabbed his neck. He raised the mutilated head and started banging it against the ground.

"Ah tell 'em. Ah tell 'em!" Propface coughed out the words over and over until Fish finally stopped. They lay next to each other, panting. Fish got on his knees and stayed in a crouch until he had caught his breath. Then he crawled through the sand creepers down to the pier and unlocked his supply crate. From a tackle box nailed to the bottom of the crate he took out his passport and other papers wrapped in plastic. He slid Toby's money in with the papers. The sub was motionless on the flat water, its hatch still flipped open. With a small pail he scooped out the water that had sloshed into *Adeline* when she overturned. In the moonlight he thought maybe the water had the tint of Sylvia's blood. He wriggled into the hull to pull out an air tank and replaced it with another from the supply crate. A spare battery pegged the amp meter, and he switched it for the one in the sub. There was no more fresh CO_2 absorbent. He hoped there would be enough left over in the onboard matrix.

Fish looked over his shoulder as he stood in the open hatch. He heard Propface muttering to himself, but he saw nothing on the dark shore. He checked the hinge and the seal on the hatch, pushed off from the pier, lowered himself in, and clamped the steel disk shut. Inside, the smell of Sylvia's vomit was faint, but persistent.

Fish twisted the ballast valves just enough to sink the wings and hull so that the small propellers were below the waterline. *Adeline* eased out into the shallows, showing only her two steel heads. She was slow and it took her an hour to reach the mouth of the elongated cove. Fish then put her into a shallow dive that pressed his shoulders against the familiar hard rim of the tower encircling his head. His eyes adjusted to the faint moonlight glow that penetrated the water around him in dim streaks. His mind was filled with faces. Sylvia laughing. Rolf staring at him. The sneering uniformed man. Big Toby shouting. Propface. Sylvia on the pallet.

He thought about making a deep dive. He could take *Adeline* down for one last look. He could take her down deeper than ever before. And then what? Quit this good and gracious life.

His lips pulled back in an involuntary grimace; he was on the verge of crying, but he forced himself not to. He tilted the sub and angled off toward a coral-studded stretch of the wall a few miles to the northeast that drew the big, double-deck dive boats from far away, their cabins full of foreigners in search of beauty. They would be there at sunrise. Fish adjusted the propeller speeds to put *Adeline* on the right heading, and as he took a deep breath, he shivered. He realized he was cold and that his clothes had absorbed all the water that he had not been able to purge from the hull. The vomit odor was nauseating. He heard a motorboat's engine pass over three times, though he never could catch a glimpse of it through the near-blackness at that depth. The night seemed to go on forever. He was very cold and yet so sleepy.

Fish woke up when his head knocked against the sharp edge of the porthole in front of his face. He was gasping; he knew he must be breathing his own carbon dioxide. He reached forward, running his hand along his leg, groping for the ballast valves. He concentrated on making his fingers move. The valves hissed and *Adeline* tilted her nose up as Fish drifted in and out of fainting. His face hit the porthole again when *Adeline* broke through the surface and flattened out on the water in a sharp slap. With trembling fingers he felt above his head for the hatch wheel and turned it slowly, his hands numb and clumsy. The lid was heavy against his palm as he tried and failed to push it up. He managed only to wedge his fingers through the seal and raise himself high enough to pull air into his nostrils through the narrow gap.

After several breaths he got the hatch open and breathed some more and struggled out. He sat astride the yellow hull, squinting at the purple fringe of the arriving dawn. He took in more air and rocked gently as *Adeline* lulled between his legs.

The dive boats came and anchored, and Fish had his choice of them. He swam toward the largest one after he had climbed back into *Adeline*, twisted the ballast valves, and let her descend with the hatch open. His body was tugged backward for a moment by the whirlpool that formed when she submerged with a slurping sound, but he stroked against the pull and kept his eyes fixed forward. Fish was counting the seconds as he approached the dive boat's ladder, and by the time he climbed aboard, he estimated that *Adeline* was already past a thousand feet, unless the fluid drag on her wings was causing her to flutter as she made her way to the bottom, passing by deep-sea lilies and other creatures rarely, if ever, seen by humans.

Victor Robert Lee writes on the Asia–Pacific region and is the author of the literary espionage novel *Performance Anomalies*, described by *The Japan Times* as "a thoroughly original work of fiction" and by Singapore's *Best of Talking Books* as "un-put-down-able." His reporting from the South China Sea and other parts of Asia can be found in *The Diplomat* and elsewhere. His reporting has been cited by *The Guardian*, BBC News, CNN, *The Economist*, *Mainichi Shimbun*, *The Singapore Straits Times*, *Asahi Shimbun*, *Bloomberg View*, *The Wall Street Journal*, *The Washington Post*, *The Week*, *National Geographic*, and other media, and in hearings of the US Senate Committee on Foreign Relations. Victor Robert Lee uses a pen name to avoid being denied travel visas by authoritarian governments.

www.victor-robert-lee.com